The Keeper's Light

A Monolith Story

By Ruel Knudson

For Grace

ISBN: 979-8-9902507-5-8 (paperback)
ISBN: 979-8-9902507-6-5 (hardcover)
ISBN: 979-8-9902507-4-1 (ebook)

Printed in the United States of America

Contents

Winter

The Keeper

The old man lay in the narrow purgatory between sleep and the waking world. It was an ethereal hour, where time had no meaning and his place in it was irrelevant.

The fireplace was cold, with only a few remnant coals still glowing dull and flat, their light and warmth all but spent. The wood shutters of the windows clacked softly as night breezes blew past them. They held back the cold fingers of the sea air, and this was good. But they kept him sequestered from the moon and the stars, the silent proclaimers of the passage of the hours, where the world sat in the cosmic clock that ticked past them all. Even the night noises were all but still. Only the rumble of the sea, which tossed itself against the rocky shore only yards from his small hovel, spoke of a world outside.

He closed his eyes and drifted back into the dark silence, existing in the vague netherworld of unsleeping. In this nebulous existence he was a thing floating in his own wandering thoughts. Consciousness released its grip, its fog-like hands drawing away from him as he sank back into the warm nothingness.

In the dark quiet came a soft, caressing song. It pulled at him, gently, but with the firm persistence of a thing that would not be denied.

It existed outside of the void, her faint gentle voice that he loved more than any other.

He smiled at the sound but did not allow it to wake him. He was afraid for it. If he did wake, it might disappear, drifting away on the receding tide of his dreaming mind. He could not bear it. He wanted to hear it, even here, lost in the places the world descends into when the mind drifts toward slumber. But another part of him knew he was not dreaming. He was aware her voice came from the waking world, filling the small room of the hovel with its melody.

His mind began to claw back into waking life. It was difficult work. His body was tired, and it refused to give up its much needed, much deserved rest. Besides, the song, the lullaby, might only be the fragmented tethers of a dream he had not been able to sink fully into. If he woke, the broken spell might end the fantasy, silencing the song once again. It had been so long, so many years since he had last heard her voice. He could not risk losing it again.

There was a desire for the rules of the waking world to assert themselves, to return to the consistent and predictable. His rational mind wanted an end to her impossible voice. There was a fear which could be banished only if reality could return to a recognizable form. It was the part of his mind craving the safety of normalcy, a gnawing need for a stable foundation of actuality which was eating away at him.

Fear wanted to take control. He was no longer easing slowly into wakefulness. He had begun to frantically pull himself through the murk, like a drowning man swimming against the riptide of his own mind. He wanted to breach the surface and escape the dream before he was pulled into its depths forever. He needed to know the lullaby was just a sad lingering memory masquerading as a figment in his sleeping imagination. If he could pull himself to wakefulness, the song would be silenced again, and the world would be as it once was – firmly and undeniably real.

When he forced himself awake, it was like opening a window onto the cold rain. The world around him came into focus with a sudden and utterly vivid clarity. He pushed himself up onto one arm and looked around the dark room suspiciously. His gaze locked on the place where she would be if the song had been more than a dream.

It was empty and silent, another vacant corner filled only with dark shadows and dust. But he thought he could hear something. No, it wasn't the song. The song had ended, and the memory of those last notes dissolved away as the fog of sleep evaporated. What he thought he could hear was a soft and muffled weeping.

He sat up fully, his threadbare blanket falling to the dusty ground. The cold sweat from his panicked skirmish with oblivion grabbed the cold air and stabbed at him with a hundred icy needles. He ignored the cold. It was nothing more than an old and persistent enemy he had long learned to tolerate.

He strained his ears for the lost voice. He heard only the wind, the rumble of the sea, and the clacking sound of the wood shutters dancing in the night air. He let out a breath and hung his head in silent disappointment. It *was* only a dream. But deep inside the lonely part of him, where he held her memory close, he wanted it to be true, despite the better reason of his mind.

He sighed deeply, frustrated by the imaginary phantom, and resolved to return to sleep. As he exhaled, a sharp and twisting pain surged through his chest. A violent fit of wet coughing doubled him over as he spat muddy phlegm into his open hand. Disgusted by the foul thing, he rubbed it away on the post of his bed. He spat out the remaining mucus onto the floor and wiped his mouth.

When the fit had passed, he cleared his throat. He leaned forward, his arms dangling between old, withered legs, taking a few moments for his breathing to calm itself. He hated this feeling. He hated it more now because it seemed to be getting worse.

Finally, he lay down and stared into the empty darkness of the rafters. He closed his eyes and drifted into a dreamless sleep.

Benjamin

The quiet hours in the early morning of the sleepy seaside village is the province of the unremarkable. The light snow drifted silently as the wind carried it from its thin rest, the sea murmured calmly, and the wispy strands of cotton clouds sailed mutely against a brilliant blue canopy. The isolated denizens with the fortitude to brave the cold tested the morning air with fragile courage. Inevitably, the unrelenting work ethic and stoic pride would win out, and the grumbling villagers would bundle themselves in layers of wool and fur before stepping out into the unpleasantly cold morning.

The normally sleepy scene was violently broken when a young man, barely twenty, came crashing through the cobbled main avenue in a full run. The older folk, who were the most eager to defy the weather in their stubborn and relentless way, watched him charge down the road with the spirited recklessness of youth. Most simply grunted and moved along. Others smiled, remembering those heady days when everything was important, and nothing could wait for the slow and deliberate walk of the self-controlled. On most days, they would catalog the event for those idle chats when resting between tasks. However, today would be different. Even the sight of the young miller tearing through the main street at a full run was far from the strangest thing they would see that day. No, today's gossip would be about the obelisk floating in the sky above the western mountains.

The emergence of this great white monolith hovering impossibly in the sky spurred the young miller through the streets as he raced to the lighthouse. He leaned into the final curve which took him off the main road and up a haphazard collection of rocky steps. He bounced up the steps, nearly clipping his booted toes against a jutting stone, and stopped in front of a flat, thatch-roofed old hovel. This was the lighthouse keeper's home, his uncle's house.

He took a moment to gather his breath. He stood there, panting hoarsely, flushed and sweating in the cold morning, waiting for his galloping lungs to reign themselves in. Once he had himself under control, he raised his hand and hammered on the door with accidental aggression. By the time he heard the annoyed grunts from inside, the soft flesh on his palm was red and raw.

He waited for seconds which seemed like hours. The door had not opened, and the gruff voice from inside had not bid him enter. He raised his fist again to deliver another round of knocking when the half-rotted wood squealed open. In the few inches afforded by the opening, the cracked and weathered face of his uncle appeared, with great bushy brows furrowed in an aggravated scowl. Recognition lit upon his face, but it did not soften it. Instead, the eyebrows seemed to dig deeper toward his nose.

"Benji? What the hell is your problem?" the old man snarled. He kept the door only partly open, as though he would slam it closed if the young man didn't answer to his satisfaction. Ben, who hadn't been called Benji by anyone else since he was ten, pushed the door open and stepped inside. His uncle stepped back, annoyed, but not surprised. The young man had been expected.

It was dark and bitterly cold in the small house. Ben started to open some shutters to let in the morning light. Meanwhile, the old man began to sort through some small logs which he then set in the fireplace. He got the fire going with little effort. The warm flames, the morning light pouring into the windows, and the soft sounds of the nearby sea filled the old and dusty cottage with a renewed life.

"Are you feeling well, Uncle? You look like you just got out of bed." Indeed, the old man was still in his dressing gown. He looked down at himself and shrugged.

"Never mind, boy," he snapped. He turned away from his nephew to find his clothes. "I've lived through three times as many mornings as you. Don't blame me for wanting a bit of extra rest now and again. Which, I might add, I could still be enjoying if you hadn't come pounding away at my door. What's got you all in a flutter anyhow? Is it the baker's girl? Did you finally ask for her hand, or did her father laugh you out of his shop?" He turned back to his nephew, a mischievous smile crooking his mouth. Then he relaxed a bit and really seemed to see the boy for the first time. "You alright, boy? You look like you ran over here."

"I did," he replied. He couldn't help the excitement in his voice, and he was quite sure he was grinning like an idiot. "I couldn't wait. Did you see it? Its right up above Moon Crest Peak. Did you see it?"

"See what? Never mind. Whatever it is, it can wait until I've got my pants on and had a cup of coffee, can't it?" The old man turned without waiting for a reply, picked up a nearby kettle, and hooked it onto the fireplace before turning back to his nephew. His hand was held open, and he looked up at the young man expectantly. "Where's the coffee, boy?"

Ben smacked himself in the head with the palm of his hand. "Oh, I'm sorry, Uncle. It's just, well, with everything happening, it's just that..."

"Quit stammering," the old man cut him off sharply. He turned back to the fireplace and pulled an old clay jar from the mantle, looked inside, and snorted. "Well, there may be enough here. But it won't be strong. I suppose you didn't bring the tobacco neither. Nor the sugar, or the salt? Too busy with everything that's happening?" He set the jar aside and shot an accusatory look over his shoulder, before heading to the wood screen by his bed to change his clothes.

Ben ignored the rebuke and continued undaunted. "You had to have heard about it. The merchants and travelers have been talking about it for months. I thought they were just a bunch of stories."

"Talking about what? I don't talk to merchants or strangers." The old man snapped from behind the screen.

"The obelisk. They've been talking about this giant obelisk floating in the sky. They say it appeared in the West months ago and has slowly been making its way East."

"That's nonsense."

"That's what I thought. But there it is, as plain as the sun. It was there this morning, floating right above Moon Crest Peak. It must have come over the mountains during the night."

"You saw it?"

"Yes. Everyone can see it. You can't miss it."

"And it's because of this floating rock that you forgot the coffee?"

"Well, yes." The boy was surprised by his uncle's disinterest. He hesitated for a moment. "It's not just a floating rock. You must see it. It's amazing!"

The old man appeared from behind the screen, fastening a button at his collar. He was dressed in his customary worn breeches, stained tunic, and a worn vest. He returned to the fireplace and prepared some coffee. A fit of harsh and wet coughing stopped him for a moment. He spat a slimy brown glob into the flames before returning the kettle back on its hook. Ben stood up, concern filling his face, the obelisk forgotten. His uncle saw the worried look on the boy's face and shook a dismissive hand. "It's nothing," the old man murmured, and he handed the boy a tin cup, steam rising from the hot brown drink inside.

"You don't sound too good, Uncle. Are you ill?"

"No, It's nothing. Just a left-over cough from a bit of a cold I had caught. That's all." The old man sat down in an old chair, worn from decades of use.

"You didn't tell me you were sick," Ben said with sudden concern.

"Well, what do ya' expect? Think I should go running down the hill, cross town, and come pounding on your door to announce my illness? Think I should be reporting my condition while I'm stuck in the middle of it? No, sir. I did just fine on my own, thank you."

"No, of course not," his nephew replied with a surprising amount of embarrassment. "It's just the cough got me worried. It's pretty ugly. I haven't heard you cough like that before."

"It's cold and wet and I'm an old man living by the ocean. What do you think is going to happen? I'll catch a sniffle or a cough now and again, which is nothing to worry about. This kind of thing comes with the territory." The old man rummaged around until he found his pipe. He started to prepare it, remembered that his nephew had forgotten the tobacco, and tossed it aside angrily, cursing under his breath.

"I'm sorry, Uncle. I'll head out soon and get your things." The old man ignored him while he took a long drink from his cup. Ben sipped at his own drink and found the coffee was very weak, almost undrinkable. Shame crept on him. When it came right down to it, his uncle wanted very little. He cared for himself, and the lighthouse, without help from anyone. It was Ben who had offered to pick up the few items he brought on his weekly visits. The old man had never asked him for a thing and was always thankful for the kindness. To Ben, these few small comforts seemed so unimportant. Until now, he never realized how great a hole was left unfilled when they were forgotten.

He looked at his uncle and, for the first time, saw how sad and old he truly was. He had become a thing time had chiseled and worn into a bitter and regretful relic. But he was also kind in his strange and abrasive way. The old man was his last living connection to a part of his family which had all but died out. Furthermore, he was a man worth loving, worth appreciating, even if the rest of the world had forgotten about him. The old man, and the lighthouse he kept, were burdens on a town that wanted to forget them, to lay them aside and pretend they no longer existed. They were the artifacts of a different time, the leftovers of a world which had long moved on.

The obelisk was wondrous, strange, and new. Despite this, it was untouchable, unknowable, distant and uncaring. It didn't need him. It didn't pass its time alone, waiting, and forgotten until a once-a-week visit rounded its corner on the calendar. It wanted nothing, and it needed nothing. There was no bond connecting the two of them to loved ones lost and dearly missed. At the age of twenty, Ben was young and still new to the world. But he understood people were fragile things, and time with them was limited and uncertain. Every single moment that could be shared with a person should have meaning. It should count for something. They should count for something.

He set his cup down and stood up to leave.

"Where are you going?" the old man asked. Ben could feel it, the small unsaid thing beckoning him to stay, which needed him to know that his uncle wanted him to be there.

"I shouldn't have forgotten your things, Uncle. I'm going to head back and get them now."

"Nonsense. Show me that silly thing in the sky first. The coffee and tobacco can wait." The old man rose to his feet, grabbed a short walking stick he sometimes used in the cold mornings as a cane, and ushered his nephew through the door into the cold wet winter.

The Keeper

In the deep and silent cold of night, the old man struggled to sleep. His mind kept wandering back to the strange obelisk his nephew had revealed to him. He recalled standing in the brisk morning air, staring unbelievingly toward the west. There it gleamed in the morning light, a great white tower, floating impossibly above the snow-capped mountains in the West, stabbing into the blue sky like a sword held aloft by some invisible king.

For most of the villagers, the long miles between their borders and the footsteps of those craggy peaks seemed closer than they truly were. The old man remembered how far away the foothills stood, and further beyond were still so many long miles until a traveler would reach the mountains. He understood what the distance truly meant. When he saw the stone spike floating above the peaks, he marveled not at the strange magic holding it in the sky. No, the true miracle was the immense size of the thing. If the stories were true, and the great tower was hewn from one single slab of stone, it must have been the creation of some great sorcerer, or even an unknowable god. Its purpose was not just mysterious, its very existence defied all reason.

His nephew said the people across the western mountains had started calling it "The Finger of God." He wondered if it might be something more wonderous, or more cruel. He was afraid the name described it perfectly. It could be the broken finger of some god or titan or the colossal phallus of a celestial deity. Would that be so horrible? There was some comfort in the idea of it being created by divine will. He shuddered to think some mortal hand constructed this thing and threw it into the sky to wander unleashed across a bemused world.

He had stared at it for a long while, standing beside his nephew. It did not move. Its travel was so slow from this distance any change was imperceptible. It was silent, but the old man felt something humming inside him as he gazed upon it, as though there were a sound, a strange and whispering voice he could not hear but knew existed. He could feel the whispering touch of loss, grief, and loneliness emanating from the monolith even across so many miles. Eventually, he would need to look away, before these feelings consumed him. But for now, he could only stare at it, like a child watching the strangeness of the universe unfold before him.

Eventually, the day had to be addressed. He turned from the object in the sky to face the more terrestrial responsibilities before him. He spent the remainder of the day toiling against the seemingly endless list of mundane chores and tasks. As he worked, thoughts of the obelisk drifted from him, and were replaced with the simple thoughts focused on his labor.

But then came night. In the dark shelter of the hovel, hidden away from the sight of the floating object, he felt like he could still sense the strange humming. However, it was far more intangible and muted. He had to force himself to feel it, reaching out for it, as one might strain to hear a whisper. If he allowed himself, he could forget it existed. It became part of the night noises, falling into the rhythmic thrum of the ocean waves, or the soft groan of the wind passing through the cracks in the wall.

Eventually, its presence slid into the ambient nothingness where all other pointless sounds lived.

When sleep finally came for him, it did so gently and silently, creeping in from the dark shadows of the cluttered room. It lay over him with soothing comfort. He welcomed it. But as he sank quietly into its embrace, he began to hear the soft notes of a song fill the night air, beautiful and clear.

His eyes flashed open, and he sat up, seizing wakefulness with desperate need. He threw aside the curtain of dream fog he believed was the siren songstress from which the lullaby had come. But the song would not be banished. It was there in the room, a voice long ago silenced by time and tragedy. Those lips that formed the words, the throat that defined the pitch and tone, the lungs that breathed life into each note belonged to a woman who no longer lived.

A chill swept through the room, crawling into his bed covers and stretching up his spine, through his bones, and freezing his marrow. The room stared back at the shivering old man with cold emptiness. There, in a corner littered with the collected refuse of a dull and empty life, where shadows from the dim light of a dying fire grew deep and black, came the song.

The lighthouse keeper sank back down onto his bed, watching the emptiness in the corner sing to him in a dead woman's invisible voice. His unbelieving eyes filled with tears as his heart broke. All the while, he listened, until the voice grew quiet and soft and disappeared back into impossibility. The old man wept until sleep crept back, finally and without further disruption.

Spring

The Keeper

Through the cold and damp winter nights the old man listened for the return of the soft lullaby sung by the unseen ghost of his long dead wife. At first, he would wait and hope the voice would not come back, that it was only a dream, some cruel trick played on him by a descent into the withering senility of old age. But she did return, every night.

In those early days, a part of him denied the reality of the visits. He did not believe in ghosts, phantasms, or fairy stories. The monsters under the bed or hiding in lightless corners were not goblins or trolls. They were the vivid creations of childhood fantasies trying to make sense of the dread they felt in their own dark loneliness. Dead things were gone and did not trouble the living.

And yet, there were such things as large stone monoliths that hover over mountaintops in the bright blue sky.

His old understanding of the world disintegrated with the arrival of the floating obelisk. The great white shining tower of stone sitting high in the nothingness had redefined what could be real. In this new world, the possibility of his wife's spirit returning to mourn their child was not so unbelievable. More importantly, he wanted it to be true. He wanted his doubt erased by the monolith, which gave silent testimony to the truth that there were no impossibilities. And if all things were possible, couldn't she be real?

Emboldened by such thoughts and ignoring the daily toil that would normally curse him with overwhelming weariness, he sat awake waiting earnestly for the first soft and tentative notes to break the stillness. He listened with rapt enthrallment as her voice grew and filled the room. He leaned forward, drawing himself closer and closer to the empty space where she sang. Tears burned the corners of his eyes before leaking down his cracked and weathered face. Then, as the voice began to fade, he fell back against his bed and wept openly and fully, hating and loving her return in equal measure.

And then one night he heard something else for the first time, a soft weeping.

She had been doing this for days before he noticed it. In those first few nights the sound had been hidden behind his own lamentation. He could not know the lullaby, which had faded into a calm silence, had grown since the initial dreamlike visit. With each new rise of the moon, she lasted just a bit longer, the inevitable fade to quiet falling later and holding on for just a few seconds more. Her presence had been growing in strength with the passing of time. Her song now continued into her own gentle sobs, aching with unquenchable grief.

Weeks passed, and winter gave way to spring. The new season came slowly. The crust of the last late snow retreated, revealing the wet ruin of last year's verdant summer. Defiantly, the first green sprigs of life popped out among the muddy brown desolation. Color returned to the world. In this time of new beginnings, the old man spent his days in the thankless continuation of his labors. The monotony was broken only by the weekly visits of his nephew. Otherwise, the old man remained oblivious to the changes around him.

He continued his vigil, marking the growing duration of her visits. He became a master of each moment, knowing through familiarity when each note might falter, or when a breath was caught in anticipation of another verse. He knew precisely when the song would end and where the weeping would begin. He catalogued her sorrow in a mental journal that noted each rise and fall, every ragged breath, and all the slow cracks spreading across her heart before it shattered into a thousand pieces. And like her singing, there was a point when this part of the cycle would end. However, instead of transitioning into something else, the room fell into empty silence.

Despite his weariness, the illness, and the heaviness of his heart, he sat in his bed listening to the last trailing sounds of his wife's sadness. For several heartbeats he would simply lay there, clinging to those last fragments. Nothing new followed, and he began to think her visits would never last any longer. He started to wonder if what he was experiencing might be some lingering essence of her last days. And behind that question came another. Why was he experiencing this now? Had the obelisk summoned her, or was it amplifying the anguish which had somehow scarred these walls? Or was his own illness driving him mad, its festering poison spreading from his lungs upward into his mind?

He eventually accepted there would be nothing more to these visits. He would only wait a few minutes more each night before finally allowing himself to fall asleep. For three days he did this, until a new sound broke the stillness in the small hovel.

His eyes flashed open. He sat up and peered into the blackness. Only silence followed. What he had heard was a solitary thing, and he thought to himself it may have been nothing more than another idle noise made by the old house. But in his heart, he was sure he heard it, and he knew it had come from her, the sound of wood creaking.

The next evening, he sat on his bed while a single candle's soft light filled the room. He waited, listening, all senses sharpened to a hunter's edge. There was no sound hidden from him. Not even the soft padded drip of the melting candle could escape those searching ears. The minutes dragged on for an eternity. Through this he waited hopefully, with quietly bated breath.

Then it came, a single sharp wooden creak that split through the air and all expectations.

This time, it was even more distinct. It was the unmistakable sound of wood rubbing against itself, pushed by some unseen hand as it rested against an invisible frame. He knew the noise, the sound, and its place in the entire theater of this haunting. This was no lingering essence. This was not the stagnant scar of an old wound trying to open itself. This was a moment in time, reliving itself, revealing itself.

For the first time since the visits started, he called out to her. He was reluctant to do this. In some way he feared his own voice might break the spell. The thought of losing these visits, of living without her, was unbearable. But this time he could not refuse the need to reach out. His voice cracked and stammered as the words caught in his throat. He tried again, little more than a whisper, but clean and clear.

Only the deep emptiness answered him.

The following morning, he returned to the lighthouse. On the ground floor, there was a large storeroom where the lumber and logs once used as fuel were kept. The lighthouse was all but retired, and its storerooms were no longer needed. The wood still stored there would continue to rot and decay as it lay unused.

The lighthouse had become another disregarded thing. Now it was only cared for by an old man who loved his wife too much to let it fall into neglect and ruin. Its only purpose was to be a vault dedicated to her memory. In its storeroom were kept all the things the old man could not bear to see, but could not bring himself to forget. The memories connected to these artifacts were beautiful and painful - and best left in this lightless dungeon where they could do him no harm.

Most of the items in the collection had belonged to his wife, or evoked remembrance of her and their life together. There was a great ornate chest filled with clothes and unfinished knitting. He found a small case with letters they had written each other before their marriage, and a meager few written after. There were many other forgotten things stored there. They had haunted the house after her death and he had chosen to bury them here. He fought back against the relentless tide of memory as he took each treasure and set it aside, pushing ever deeper into the dismissed remains of their life together.

Finally, he came to it. Tucked in the corner, neatly barricaded by the last evidence of her mortal existence, was the battered and worn bassinet of the child who never lived. This was the object of his search. It was a small and pitiful thing. The wood was beginning to show signs of rot. It had no bedding. It was nothing more than the skeletal carcass of their combined hopes, a dream that died too quickly and too abruptly.

He knelt beside it, examining it, searching its moldering structure. He ran his fingers across the rough wood and rusted nails. He could remember selecting each piece of the frame, carving, and bending the wood to his exact need. The iron nails in the frame had been driven in by a hammer wielded in his hand. The cradle was theirs, but he was the craftsman who lovingly built it for a child who would never take a living breath.

The deep emptiness of the lonely years without them seemed to bear down on him. He leaned forward, resting his hand on the frame. He allowed the weakened wood to take only a little of his weight. He only needed a little help to ease the heaviness in his heart. But it was enough for the bassinet to resist, and he heard a small and familiar creak of wood rubbing against wood.

Benjamin

The obelisk continued its silent disinterested march eastward. It was essentially doing nothing more than floating indifferently on the horizon. It was another feature in the sky with no more influence on them than the mountains over which it hovered. Even its progress was so utterly slow, no one could see it was growing closer with each passing day. In fact, if someone had the interest, and the skill, they could have measured its apparent size and been able to deduce how close it would come to their village and when. Such a person may have determined that by the middle of summer, the tower would pass close enough for its great shadow to drift across the farms and fields like a giant sundial.

No one had the foresight, or for that matter the interest to predict the obelisk's path. Since the object did nothing, it had in time been dismissed and forgotten. It was no more important than the moon in the night sky, a curious and beautiful oddity with little useful purpose, except to those who wanted to imagine some hidden power behind it. To the average person, it was nothing more than a meaningless ornament shining in the sky.

But this was a whole new world for Ben. There was a time when the obelisk added something magical and boundless to their staid and unchanging lives. In those first days there was an electric giddiness throughout the village and farms. Its sudden arrival was a heady intoxicant which seemed to have some profound effects on the population. But this power was short-lived, owing only to the arrival of something strange and new, and not by some mystic property attributed to the object itself.

There was a wide mixture of reactions in those early days. Some people were fearful of the monolith and believed it was a portent of a coming doom. For others, it was the herald of unexpected change. There was a great settling of old debts and of making old wrongs right. Metaphorical fences were mended. Burnt bridges were made new again. People came together in forgiveness with old transgressions pardoned. It was a time to prepare for whatever great future might be coming, and they did not want to be burdened by ill feeling and old grudges.

A small few began to hoard food, medicine, and sundries in even greater store than winter required. These poor fools severed old bonds, abandoned lifelong friendships, and assigned family members a value based only on their closeness by blood or ambiguously perceived usefulness. They retreated from the world in irrational fear. The obelisk was terrifying in its abject disregard for the laws of the real world as it hung in the sky, in direct mockery of the gods and all that was good. These few feared monstrous demons might come in the wake of the great stone tower to burn, rape, and kill all who fell under its shadow.

Within weeks, the better and more rational nature of the people took over. No demons came forth from the bowels of Hell. The only warm days ahead of them were those which fell behind the turning of winter into spring. Aside from the fact the obelisk existed, there was no difference in the world from the day before it arrived and the days that followed.

There was also the curious effect of the sudden scheduling of spring weddings. Even Ben, after many years of silent adoration, was filled with careless confidence. He pronounced his love to the baker's daughter, and with her father's blessing, asked her to marry him. Maybe it was the heady nectar of this new world where giant white stone pillars flew across mountains, but he was not surprised when she said yes.

In the midst of spring, and only a day until his wedding (one of three that week), the young miller made the journey down the main avenue, a blissful and stupid grin beaming on a face tilted ever so slightly to catch the warm rays of the morning sun. He arrived at the aged wood door of his uncle's hovel and was about to raise a hand to knock, when he was stopped by a loud and brittle-sounding cough coming from around the back of the house where the path led to the lighthouse.

He followed the narrow footpath of crushed shells winding its short, forty-meter distance through the jutting rocks to the stone bridge sticking out of the cliff like a great, gray finger. The end of the bridge was connected to a protrusion of jagged cliff. Built into the crags, as though it emerged from those rocks, stood the lighthouse.

It was a short and squat tower of dark gray and black brick standing only four stories high. It was built in ancient days before lenses or polished mirrors. Its only light was essentially a great bonfire which would be lit at its top, if such a need were to rise again. Its roof, where the fire would burn in those ancient times, was little more than a crown of crenelated stone, its upper teeth rounded at the caps. Many of these were topped with the white dripping stains of gull droppings. Some of these flying vandals circled above, while others pranced upon the stone tops mewing at each other aggravatingly. There were only a few narrow windows in the old tower. Some might face the sea, but Ben could not see those. The windows facing the walkway stood like slender slits of spider eyes. Below the vertical gashes was a great wooden door left partially open, its wood cracked and softened near the bottom with rot.

Ben crossed the bridge. It was wide enough for a cart, and he supposed this was to facilitate the delivery of wood logs and other fuel for the bonfire. There were wood posts at each end of the walkway linked together by a thick iron chain, marred and pitted with rust, hanging low and neglected. It swung back and forth in the breeze, squeaking slightly in a soft and comforting rhythm. Below him, the sea frothed in a foaming soup, and he could smell the spray of the waves as they smashed against the wall of rock.

He rarely came to the lighthouse. The tower always seemed to loom over him. Its presence grew more ominous as he crossed the bridge, pressing at him, while the sea below was reaching up for him in futile grasping fingers, wanting to pull him down and into its cold embrace. He shook away these childhood fears. It was only a lighthouse, his family's lighthouse, whom his aunt had inherited, and her widower now kept as his own burden. What its future might be, when his uncle relented his charge, he could not know. By rights, it fell to him, the last of his aunt's family left living. But, the old tower no longer had a purpose, and his own life was filling with new responsibility.

Another cough made him look up. Ben could see his uncle through the open door, rummaging inside. As he finished crossing the bridge and approached the tower door, he caught a tirade of frustrated curses explode from the old man and echo around the inner chamber. Ben decided it would be best to wait at the doorway instead of entering.

He watched as the old man secured a large door with a key, which he promptly dropped into a vest pocket. Another brief fit of coughing stopped him for a few seconds. Ben was becoming more concerned about this persistent illness. As he watched him, his fears were confirmed. His uncle looked more ragged and worn out. Normally he could be described as wiry and thin. Now he almost looked too thin. More than anything, he looked tired. Deep shadows filled around his eyes, and his normally purposeful stride was becoming a slow shuffle. He clearly needed a good rest, maybe a long sleep. Ben wondered if the illness was keeping him awake at night. He struggled with how he would confront the old man about it. The last time he tried, his uncle had snapped back at him angrily, dismissing his concerns with an outburst of very colorful curses. He would have to be more diplomatic this time and wait for an opportunity.

Once his uncle had recovered himself, he looked up and spotted his nephew leaning against the doorframe. He turned away, spat onto the floor, and wiped his mouth on his sleeve. Finally, he turned back and waved his nephew inside.

"Good morning, Uncle," Ben greeted as he entered the chamber. His voice bounced around the empty space, echoing off the stone walls in a sudden burst of sound. He was surprised by this and looked around the room as though his eyes were following the dancing voice.

"It's about time you got here. Where've you been? Never mind. You're in time to help me get this to the house." The old man motioned to a large wooden chest he had excavated from the locked room.

"What is it?" Ben asked. It was a large chest, with beautifully carved swirls flowing around it, like waves curling over each other. Above the swirls were flowing lines which followed the crests of the waves, broken only by the rare addition of carved birds, their wings opened wide as if receiving the flowing lines. He set the wrapped bundle he had brought for his uncle aside and knelt in front of the chest, tracing the intricate lines with his fingers. "It's beautiful," he whispered.

"It's a wedding present." His uncle replied. His face was filled with silent pride as he watched his nephew admire the chest. Ben looked up at the old man, surprised.

"Uncle, you don't have to do that. Honestly, I'm truly just happy you're going to be at the wedding. This," he paused. He didn't want his uncle to feel like he was rejecting the gift. On the contrary, it was beautiful, and he could only imagine how his new wife would love it. But he also knew it once belonged to his aunt. This was a treasure among treasures. He hated the idea of separating his uncle from anything which had once been hers.

"Stop it, boy." He coughed again. It was small and sharp, more of an aftershock of his last explosive outburst. It was no less concerning to Ben, but the old man continued before his nephew could say anything about it. "There's not much there. Just a few things. Your aunt's things. Her old clothes, some other things she wore, hats, and shawls and the like. It isn't much, but it's not doing me any good. Besides, I'd not be surprised to find most of it is moth ridden or rotten. I'll pull out what's no good. If nothing survives, well, you'll have a pretty enough box, I guess."

Ben hadn't considered there would be anything inside the chest. He was overwhelmed by the gift. The thought his uncle was passing something so connected to her, and bequeathing them to his wife, was more than Ben had ever expected. He stood up, and to his uncle's surprise, wrapped his arms around the old man in a firm and loving hug.

His uncle allowed him a brief few seconds before peeling himself out of the embrace. His face was red from embarrassment, but his eyes were wet with emotion.

"She's going to love it," Ben finally confessed, a strange lump in his throat choking the words into a chalky mess.

"I'm sure," Uncle replied, trying to move on from the awkwardness he clearly hadn't been ready for. "Your aunt had wonderful taste in fabric. She was a fine hand with a needle and thread too. She made most of the stuff in there herself. Well, a few things I'm sure your own mother helped with." He looked down at the chest with a troubled look, rubbing the back of his neck. "I sure hope some of those old clothes survived. They sure were pretty on her. I think it would make her happy to know her fine work was going to that lovely wife of yours." The old man smiled weakly; his eyes seemed far away as he looked back into the past.

Ben allowed his uncle to have a few seconds of reflection. Then he reached down and wrapped his hands around one of the knotted ropes that was used as a handle. With his free hand he gathered the package he had brought. Then, he lifted the chest and looked back to his uncle. "Ready?"

The old man seemed to break free from the memories, smiled awkwardly, and grabbed the rope handle on the other side of the chest. "Get on with you, Benji."

As they crossed the bridge, Ben figured it was a good enough time to bring up the package he was carrying. He held it up with his free hand. "I almost forgot about this. All the usual stuff is in there. I also added some tea, and thyme. It should help with your cough. At least, I hope you'll try it."

The old man snorted dismissively. "The cough ain't nothing. You worry about your wedding and don't bother with me. It's just a bit of the old cold anyhow."

"I don't think so," the young man argued. "You've been sitting on that cough for weeks now. At least give the tea a try." They arrived at the hovel, entered, and set the chest down on the floor while Ben continued. "Look, you've already had your morning coffee. I'll get the kettle started and you can try some of the thyme. Consider it a wedding present."

"I thought your aunt's old chest was a good enough wedding present. Had you all misty-eyed," mocked the old man. He grabbed a small bag of tobacco from the open package of goods and retrieved his pipe from the mantle. He sat down and stole a glance at his nephew. Ben flashed a sharp look at him, his eyes sharp and dagger like. The old man waved him off with a mischievous smile and started to pack his pipe with some fresh tobacco. His nephew continued to prepare the kettle. Then he noticed something in the old house which hadn't been there on his last visit.

"What's this?"

"What's what?" his uncle asked as he stuck a small stick into the fire to heat the tip. He promptly brought the flame-touched end to his pipe and lit the bowl. A few sharp puffs and he sat back, apparently satisfied with his effort.

"This?" Ben tapped the rickety wood of an old bassinet. "Are you expecting, Uncle?"

The old man looked at him, raised the pipe to his mouth, and inhaled a long slow draw. The timing seemed suspicious, as though he had caught the old man off guard, and he was only using the pipe to give himself enough time to think of an explanation. Maybe his uncle hadn't meant for him to see it. The old man released a slow stream of smoke before he answered.

"I found it when I went looking for the trunk. I thought maybe I could fix it up. You know, in case you might be wanting it."

Ben chuckled awkwardly. "Well, I appreciate the thought. But I think it's a bit early. The wedding's tomorrow. We won't be needing it for a little bit longer, I hope. Otherwise, she'll have some explaining to do."

"Don't be stupid, Benji," he snapped. "It's pretty far gone. It'll take a while to fix the rotten wood. I just figured I could get an early start on it." His uncle's face had darkened. Ben had almost forgotten about the child his aunt and uncle had lost. He began to understand the room was filling up with reminders of this heartache. His uncle's greatest pain was on full display, and he had been cracking jokes about it.

"I'm sorry," was all he could say. The apology felt weak. He tried to move beyond it. "You just surprised me. You know, I hadn't really thought of children before now. I was just sort of caught up in the getting married part."

"Well, you should think about them. They sneak up on you. Better to have it ready, and not need it..." he stopped himself before going any further. The thought hovered in the air, unspoken, but still very loudly said. The sudden memories washed over the wrinkled face like a liquid shadow. Ben fiddled absently with the firewood as he thought of something to banish the uncomfortable cloud gathering in the room.

"Would you be willing to let me help you out with the bassinet when I come for my visits?"

His uncle's face brightened at this. "I thought those might start slowing down after you got married."

Ben brought the cups down off the mantle and lifted the kettle to fill them. The smell of the tea started to fill the room. "Sorry, Uncle. You're still going to have to make room in your busy schedule for me to stop by once a week. Just you and me, mind you. I don't want Lilia getting nervous and thinking about leaving me on account of you being a bad host."

"Shut up. You're an ungrateful runt, you know that?" he retorted through teeth clenched tight around his pipe. But the dark cloud which had been filling the house was thinning and being replaced with the comfortable warmth of their usual back and forth. The old man had an uncharacteristic grin which held up even when Ben handed him a cup of the god-awful tea.

Summer

The Keeper

In the growing heat of long summer days, the ocean breeze brought a welcome relief for the lighthouse keeper. He often left the shutters open, even into the night. The cool wind was lightly spiced with the fresh salty scent of the nearby sea, whose gentle rumble rolled freely into the open windows of the hovel. Moonlight cast the room in a soft luminous shine, giving the world a dreamlike glow.

The old man sat quietly near the fireplace. He was immune to the romantic lure of the scene and its quiet and haunting serenity. He sat as he had sat each night since spring, little more than another old and broken curiosity in the cluttered home. His eyes were fixed firmly on the bassinet, now showing the care and love Benji and he had put into repairing it. There was an eager anticipation in his eyes. They gleamed hopefully, but there was also the light of earnest madness in them, a greedy spark touching the middle of his irises. He was frozen and unmoving. If a coughing fit would take him, he would simply accept it and spit the dislodged phlegm into the fireplace before returning his gaze back to the bassinet with almost mechanical accuracy.

The whole world started there, in that small dark corner of the room. For a few hours every night, nothing at all mattered except for those moments when she would arrive. It would never change, yet it always became more. He would listen to the familiar song, the weeping which followed, and the sounds of her movement as she rose unseen from the bassinet. Each day a new moment was added to the play. Eventually, the metal hinges of the front door would groan as its spectral counterpart would open. He would follow her out of the house and along the path of crushed shells toward the lighthouse, guided only by the soft shuffle of her invisible feet and her sporadic and incoherent muttering. Then those sounds would also stop, though always a few feet further along the path to the lighthouse, where he expected he would soon hear those doors open.

After the sounds of his wife drifted away, he would stand and wait for some other sign of her presence. Perhaps she had only stopped walking, paused her muttering, and was waiting herself. In those moments he would often look at the great white obelisk, glowing in the reflected moonlight, as it hovered there among the stars just to the south. It was eerie in its utter silence, its unwillingness to reveal anything about itself. Benji had said some people refused to leave their homes when its shadow crossed their land. The lightkeeper thought this was absurd. The giant structure was harmless. It had no will. Its shadow had no influence. He knew there was power in the obelisk. He was certain its appearance, and its time in the sky, was somehow responsible for the nightly presence of his wife. How or why did not matter. He only looked up at the Finger of God with a thankful heart. If he feared anything, it was the monolith's inevitable passing into the east, where it would fall into the horizon. He was afraid once it was gone, the power which allowed his beloved to return to him would disappear as well.

While the obelisk traveled slowly across the sky, it remained otherwise unchanged. It still hovered mutely in the sky, indifferent to the old man watching it with growing fear of its passing. Even the soft droning hum was consistent and monotonous. It had effectively become such a constant part of his life he had to concentrate to notice it.

Meanwhile, his wife's visits would persist and grow longer each day, as they had since she first came to him in the night. Like the obelisk's slow journey toward some final and unknown conclusion, these visits persisted with the unhurried pace of the inevitable. But during those early days the haunting spirit of the lightkeeper's wife had only been the sad echo of her voice. In the spring, he had come to realize it was so much more. The sounds of her movement told him he was really listening to an instance in time. Either she was trapped here, reliving this moment each night, or returning just to touch the living world again.

He wanted to believe this was not just some empty echo of what had been. He felt there was some greater purpose to this. If it were true, then this wasn't just a meaningless reflection, but a specific episode in her life, probably her last moments. He was afraid of this, but he also felt a strange need to understand it, to be there for it. Furthermore, there was a growing sense of being together with her, as though her presence was a connection to him that was slowly knitting itself back together.

The last time he could remember feeling this was just after her death. He had often dreamt of her then. In those dreams, it was as if she had not died at all. Their lives, in whatever strange and euphoric version he could imagine at the time, was lived in the comfortable surety that they were whole, and together. The illusion would be destroyed upon waking. Each morning had been like reliving her passing all over again, with all the pain and sadness flooding back as a terrible reminder of the truth.

Eventually the sadness had diminished, and he had started hoping for the dreams. Those small bits of connection were only fantasy, but during the dreams, they were completely real. He learned to treasure those illusions. Even her memory faded in time. But the dreams, those magical visions, were real in ways his memories were not. In those dreams he had been able to hold her again, kiss her again, be in love with her again.

For the rest of his life, he would dream of her. But those nights were fewer and further apart. He had come to a point in his acceptance of her passing where he welcomed the dreams, and he would wake without the sadness.

These nightly visits had been like those dreams after her passing. Night after night she haunted him, breaking his heart, causing him to mourn her death again and again. Now, in the fullness of summer, he began to accept them, accept her, as a new blessing. He could not hold her; he could not kiss her. If he spoke to her, his voice would not be heard. But he was with her. Or rather, she was here with him. Somehow, it was enough, and he did not want it to end.

The connection to the presence of the obelisk, and its arrival at the nearest most point to the lighthouse in its voyage, may have been a greater influence than the old man had anticipated. Or perhaps, as the old wise women would often say, there was a power in the solstice which gave strength to some fey magic that weakens the barrier between the living and the dead. For it was on Midsummer's Eve when he first saw her manifest before his eyes. As she sang the nightly lullaby, he watched in wonder as the apparition took form, like thin wisps of otherworldly smoke slowly gathering itself into the singular perfect image of her. She knelt with a hand resting lightly on the bassinet, her face full of grief as she reached into the basket.

Her song ended, and her head slumped down as her shoulders began to shudder. He knelt beside her. His trembling hand reached for her. Instead of touching her soft shoulder, his fingers simply passed through her. She was only light, and nothing more, and the light was beginning to fade. He called out to her, beckoning to her. She did not look up. She only wept and slowly vanished.

He did not move. He sat on the floor beside her, listening to her cries. He was surprised by his own calm. He was not crying in grief, because there was no sadness in seeing her. The image moved him greatly, enforcing the feeling of connection, togetherness, in a new and amazing way. Her gloriously radiant beauty had been robbed from him for so long. It was the light of dawn after a long winter night. It banished away the darkness, bringing warmth and the promise of spring. It gave him hope.

Her image did not reappear that night. She was only the voice and sounds, once again an invisible phantom. But, on the next night, she did return, and every night thereafter. And each night her image grew stronger and more real and would last just a few moments longer than the night before.

Benjamin

Ben prepared the kettle while he waited for his uncle. The old man was changing behind the screen. A wet explosion of coughing erupted behind the partition. The old man cursed and resumed the shuffling noises as he dressed. Ben stifled an urge to say something about his uncle's health. Any conversation about the growing illness was pointless. His concern was always appreciated. Despite his fears, he was always told there was nothing to be worried about.

But something was very wrong. It had progressed beyond the relentless coughing. This was the third visit in as many weeks where Ben had woken his uncle upon arrival. Today, in fact, Ben was over two hours late. And still his uncle came to the door in his night shirt, bleary eyed and unkempt. Ben wondered how late his uncle had been sleeping on those days when Ben wasn't knocking on his door. How many mornings had the old man lost?

It wasn't just waking late which worried Ben. His uncle's current appearance was disturbing to say the least. He was always a lean man, but he looked absolutely gaunt now. His skin stretched across sharp and bony cheeks. His eyes were sunken and dark, while often glazing over and dimming in an absent and listless fog as the man stared into nothing. He was so thin now his clothes looked like they belonged to a man twice his size. They hung from him like rags, stained with sweat and mucus. Ben now made it a point to arrive with a warm meal of sausage, eggs, and bread prepared at his request by his loving wife. The old man ate sparingly but was always thankful. The weekly repast was probably not going to improve his uncle's health in any significant way. But it was worth trying something, anything.

He was dying. Ben knew it, and he thought his uncle might know it too. Neither would talk about it. Yet, it was coming. The hovel stank of it. The old man reeked of it. His eyes would brighten when he spoke and he moved without any lost effort. But he looked like a walking corpse, a thin, taut, and desiccated husk of the man he once was. He didn't think his uncle would see another summer. He was even worried the old man might not last through winter.

"Uncle, I've been thinking."

"Yeah, what about?" His voice came back sounding cracked and chalky. Another new feature brought on by the illness.

"About the lighthouse. There's talk of some folks getting a few fishing boats. Some are even saying they might be building the fleet back up. The bay's still full of fish, maybe even fuller as there haven't been any nets cast out there in quite a few years."

The old man stepped out from the screen, tying off the last few buttons. He picked up a sausage, nibbled a bit at the end and looked thoughtfully out of the window toward the lighthouse. "Well, I'd like to see it. It would be good to get some boats back out there again. Unfortunately, it won't happen. They talk about the old fleet just about every summer. Truth is, fishing is hard, and the sea is dangerous. Men go out for days sometimes, catch a little, or a lot, and sometimes they don't come back. Farming ain't so dangerous. No one goes out to get the carrots and gets lost in a storm and drowns. Besides, ain't no real sailors left around here. You get them on a boat..." he finished laughing a dry and sandy laugh while shaking his head. He picked up a sanding block and sat down next to the bassinet.

"There's a few people who still go out on the water," Ben argued.

"Yeah, on little rowboats or skiffs. They go out for a bit of fun on the water, maybe a spot of small fishing. The ships they need for proper fishing are big, needing six or more men to operate properly. Mind you, those are ships, not boats, and not but a few men, all older than me, remember how to work those. Nah, these folk will talk about it, maybe even decide to do it. But when it comes time to pull out the coin, those purses will snatch together tight, and to a single man they will think it might be something best looked at next year. It's the way it's been, and the way it will be."

"Well, it's a shame if it's true. I sure would have liked to see some of those big ships they tell the stories about."

"Yes, it was a sight," the old man said reflectively. "I was just a boy myself when the storm finished off the fleet. Keep in mind, there weren't but a handful of ships left even then. That storm, it just finished off what was already a dying thing. Too many people had picked up the plough and abandoned the sea. I guess it's sad in its own way. I don't really think so, though. It's just the way things are. Time moves on and people move with it."

"What about the lighthouse?"

The old man coughed again. It was a short burst followed by the old man spitting a fat phlegmy wad of black tar into the cold fireplace with an indifference that frightened Ben. He tried to hide his disgust and pushed the conversation forward.

"Well, I was thinking about you showing me how to tend it."

The old man's eyes narrowed suspiciously. "Why would you want to do that? Like I said, ain't no fishing boats coming back. Ain't no purpose for you keeping it."

"Well, what about..." he was unsure how to finish without insulting his uncle.

"What about when I'm too old to keep it? Sorry to say, Benji, but that time's long past. I've been too old to keep it for years. But here I am, getting ready to start another day of caring for the pointless old tower."

"Well, maybe it's time to pass the burden on to someone else. I could help at least. We can decide about taking it over completely later. Let's just see about me doing a bit here and there. How's that sound?"

The old man grunted. "It sounds about as stupid a thing as you can say. Your father, and his father before him, worked that mill and passed it down to you. It's work you like, and you're good at, more than just a bit good. You're properly good. The mill needs you, and the town needs the mill. This lighthouse ain't needed by anyone. It isn't your responsibility anyhow. So, I say no. You aren't going to learn to help out here and there. You definitely won't be taking on keeping the lighthouse. As long as I can, I'll do what I can do. After that, let the whole damned tower fall into the water for all I care."

"Uncle, be reasonable," he argued. He could see the futility in it, but he had to try. The idea of his uncle killing himself tending the tower was too much to bear. Not when he could do something about it. "It's my family's responsibility, isn't it? By rights, after my aunt died it should have fallen to me. I mean, it's only proper I should start taking care of it. Maybe I should have taken it a long time ago, and I'm sorry for that. But I want to do the right thing now."

The old man leaned forward, fury reddening his face. Ben sat back, trying to avoid the rage boiling in the old man's eyes. He lost the battle and looked down at his feet. "You want to do the right thing?" Before he could answer the old man kept going, rising out of his seat, and gesturing to the window facing the lighthouse. "You think it should have fallen to you? The damned tower was never yours, Benji. It was your aunt's. Now, you might've loved her, God knows most people did, and you're her kin. But I knew her. I knew her down to her core. And I am here to tell you, on her behalf, the lighthouse was never meant to be yours. Your aunt loved you so very much. The last thing in the world she would want is for that empty and useless pile of rocks out there to be your obligation."

"Yeah, but..."

"No!" he snapped. In a surprising display of anger, he threw the sanding block against the wall. "You don't get to throw everything away taking care of that thing. Because that's what it takes. Tending the tower ain't just sweeping cobwebs. It's work, all day, every day. There'd be no more milling for you. You and your wife would have to move in here. You'd be giving up what you got for nothing.

"You have a good life, a lovely wife, a family to start. Your milling operation has value. The lighthouse is nothing more than an old and rotted bone. Let it be buried and forget about it. Do you understand? There is no good which can come from tending the tower. So, let it die."

The old man had made his way to the window. He was looking out to the lighthouse. Ben got off his chair and stood beside him. He could see the anger in the eyes of the old man as he glared contemptuously at the tower. The only thing the tower offered him was a connection to his late wife. Aside from that sole blessing, he hated it. He hated it down to the very rock it perched on.

Ben didn't know what to say. He didn't like the idea of the old lighthouse going to ruin. However, he understood what his uncle was trying to tell him. Deep down, the idea of having to inherit the lighthouse was terrifying to him. And yet, there was a magic which still hadn't been driven from it. He wasn't sure what he wanted from the ugly tower of gray stone, but he was sure he didn't want to just let it go.

The old man seemed to sense the conflict within his nephew. His face softened and he turned away from the window and sat back down in his old chair. He took up his pipe in one hand and appeared to be inspecting it. He turned it from side to side inquisitively while mulling over some deep secret held within it. Finally, he set it down and looked up to Ben.

"I'll tell you what, Benji. When you got some time, bring a cart up here, a big one. Bring Lilia with you. That wife of yours is a fine girl, clever. You'll likely want her smarts to tell what's worth keeping. The three of us will empty out the old storeroom. You two choose what you'll save first. Afterward, I'll choose a bit for myself. Once we have what we want, we're done with the place. Both of us. We won't waste any more effort on it. We'll lock up the big doors and toss the key into the sea. No one in this family is going to put another ounce of blood or sweat into the lighthouse. Will that do for you? Will you promise me we can put the old thing to rest?"

"I promise," he replied sullenly. "But what about the stuff we don't keep?"

The old man thought about it for a moment. "We'll take it to the top. Your aunt's birthday will be coming up in the fall. We'll set it up there and light the candle for her one last time. How about that? The three of us will say goodbye to the old pile of rocks properly."

The smile which spread across Ben's face must have been broad and contagious. Even the old man smiled a bit, his eyes wide and bright. The young man's heart lifted at the very idea of seeing the lighthouse burning, even if it would be the last time. He wasn't sure if anyone still alive could remember seeing the lighthouse's fire. It had never been lit in his lifetime. As a child, he often imagined it. In those wonderful dreams he pictured a radiant torch burning bright against the black night sky. An immense red flame which danced atop the black silent sentinel and shown down on all of them like Heaven's light. Sharing such a moment with his uncle and his wife seemed like the perfect way to end the long years of burden.

"Uncle," he said, barely containing his excitement. "It sounds perfect!"

Autumn – Part 1

The Keeper

The old man's shuffling feet echoed across the naked stone of the lighthouse stairs. He made the ascent in almost complete darkness. He pressed his left hand against the cold brick wall. It was his only real guide among the small beams of silver moonlight which lanced through the southern facing windows. He had climbed these stairs almost every day for what seemed like a lifetime, but only recently had it become difficult.

His old legs shook with the strain as his joints and muscles screamed at him angrily. The greatest pain was in his lungs. The illness had done its work well, slowly killing him in its secret and thieving way. The racking coughs expelled both blood and black mucus in equal measure, assaulting him at almost every floor. He could ignore it for now. He would press ahead, accepting the strain of the labor as a matter of course, a price he would gladly pay each and every night if his strength would hold out. He needed to reach the summit, the crown of the stone tower, where he would wait for her to arrive.

He would escape into memory while making the climb. Disconnected from the tedium of the ascent, his thoughts always turned to her. He reflected on the passage of the last year, and how her nightly presence would grow in strength and clarity. In the waning summer, she became more visible, almost tangible. He would see her, at first, as she sang and wept. She would rise from the bassinet and evaporate like a mist dispersed by a strong breeze. He would then follow the sounds of her footsteps as she left the hovel and took the path of crushed shells to the lighthouse. He walked beside her unseen presence as he listened earnestly to her unintelligible whispering. Her amorphous vision appeared and crossed the narrow bridge, pausing only a moment to gaze back at the hovel with a look of sad regret.

Each night her journey would reveal a bit more. Soon she was entering the lighthouse, where she lingered only for a moment at the foot of the stairs before stepping onto them. Sometimes other images of her would appear before vanishing within the slow blink of an eye. The spectral sounds of her passage were the only unfailing companion in those cold and echoing chambers. Finally, at the end of their journey, she would make one final appearance. Her phantom would stand at the edge of the crown. She stood at the short knee-high parapet wall which guarded the fatal edge, looking out at a curtain of starlight set atop a black and rumbling sea until finally fading away into the night.

It was the brutal curse of age or illness, eating at his strength in its gluttonous way, which had finally necessitated a change in his relationship with her spirit. Her apparition, trapped in the timeless moment when she was young, had the strength and fortitude of youth the old man could no longer claim. Unable to keep pace with her, he would sit in the warmth of the hovel as a nightly witness to her visits. When she left through the front door he would follow her outside, stopping just beyond the threshold. He waited for her to appear at the bridge. He would watch as she would look back toward him, knowing she didn't see him. While it was only the reflection of a moment, another reenactment he had seen numerous times replayed without variation, he would imagine she was looking at him. He would lift his hand in a gentle wave and smile just a little bit, allowing the charade to feel real for just a heartbeat. Then she would turn and enter the lighthouse where he could no longer watch or hear her. With a cold and heavy heart, he would retire back into the small house for his nightly rest.

This concession had its own difficulties. Each night he found himself watching her leave him behind. He was confident she would return on the next night. So long as the obelisk still shone in the night sky, he felt the power which allowed her to be here would not fail him. But, there was always a savagely horrible fear it would betray him. The thought of his last sight of her, looking forlornly at him from the bridge before walking away, was terrifying. The needling fear burrowed into the weakening surety of his mind each night, growing in intensity, and becoming more rational with time. In the end, he decided what little power he did have in this arcane theater was limited to how he would participate in it. From that point on, he would wait for her at the top of the tower. They would stand, looking out at the night sky and the rumbling sea, and just be there together.

On the eve of her birthday, he made the long climb, as he had done for the past few nights. When he reached the top, he allowed himself a brief rest. The muscles in his legs were twisting in angry cramps, his lungs were on fire, and his heart was beating at a gallop. He had been coughing furiously throughout the ascent. With only a brief walk to go, he could afford a few minutes to gather his strength.

He sat down at the top and final step. His gaze was drawn to the center of the crown where Benji and Lilia had been adding to an enormous pile of discarded objects. It was junk really, a mound of refuse donated by the town for the last burning of the lighthouse's torch.

Somehow, people had heard about the light-keeper and Benji's plans. The news had awakened some nostalgic spirit within the village and its surrounding farms. Most had wanted to contribute something to the last fire. Over the course of several days, groups of people delivered small mementos and keepsakes which might have held some meaning to them in another time. But now the objects were just useless junk which they found easy to part with. Some brought small planks of wood or scrimshaw painted or carved with messages. Many of these were wishes which they hoped would be granted in some mystical way only the silly, superstitious, or stupid could understand. Others were messages of farewell to the lighthouse.

The keeper found these even more ridiculous as he was convinced the tower didn't care one bit. But, the expression touched him in strange way his normally cynical mind wanted to resist. It was the toys which seemed to be the most impressive to him. For a child, such things as dolls or carved soldiers were more than treasures. These were the sacred totems of youth. Even as age would eventually take charge and the attention they once commanded would wane, there would always be the lingering love which would never spoil. To see them among the discarded sundry in the pile spoke to him. These were hallowed relics, treasures beyond their worth. These toys were loved, and their presence was the strongest outpouring of the worthy sentiment he could imagine.

Within reaching distance of where he rested lay one of those toys. It must have tumbled from the pyre earlier, for it lay a few feet from edge of the pile, forgotten and alone. The old man leaned over, picked it up, and examined the curious thing. It was a small soldier, a knight perhaps, and it appeared to have been well loved by its former owner. Its paint was chipped and rubbed almost bare in some areas. The small sword he held was broken at the top.

It looked to have small little dents, perhaps teeth marks, from some younger brother or sister who had gotten hold of it. For a moment, he thought to keep it. It was beautiful in its scarred and worn way. But it was meant for the fire. Its previous owner had deemed it to be given to the lighthouse. Reluctantly, he tossed it back on the pile. He pulled his gaze from the mound of sentimentality and looked out to the star-speckled night sky.

His strength had returned, and he continued his course. He made his way around the edge of the ever-growing pile. Soon, it would finally be set alight. He imagined it would burn throughout the night, and perhaps into the better part of the next day. For now, he simply had to watch for any other wayward items which had fallen, like the scarred wooden toy soldier, from the impending pyre. When he found one, he picked it up and tossed it back onto the heap. Slowly and carefully, he made his way to the east side of the crenulated wall where she would appear on the final leg of her nightly journey before disappearing.

While he waited, he looked out to the obelisk. It was high and distant, a white tower shining from reflected moonlight. It hovered above the dark water in the eastern sky, its inverted reflection pointing back toward the lighthouse. Soon its long journey would take it across the horizon to parts unknown, its slow passage among the clouds nothing more than a peculiar memory. He had been afraid that once it vanished below the blue line of the sea his wife would be gone, leaving him alone with only his grief to remember her. Now he could feel the illness growing inside him. He knew, deep in his bones, it wouldn't be long before he would join her. Thus, the fate of the floating tower, and any power it had over his wife's spirit, no longer brought him any fear. Now, it was a mysterious wonder in the sky which had brought him a final amazing gift.

He turned back to the stairs so that he might witness her arrival. It was several hours past midnight, her usual hour, and her coming was imminent. He could hear the approaching steps. Even the percussion of the sea could not conceal those sounds. A thin and wavering form materialized before him. At each step the vague and amorphous shape coalesced into the full illusion of her living form. When she stopped next to him, she appeared so vividly alive he could lose himself in the delusion that he was standing beside a warm and breathing person.

Her eyes were locked to the horizon. At this point, she would linger the longest. She was radiant in the starlight with the wind from the sea blowing through her hair and the thin night dress she wore clinging to her like a second skin, its excess cloth trailing behind her with the breeze. But her face was sad and lost. A wet shine on her cheeks marked the passage of silent tears. She breathed heavy and deep, as though fighting for control in a tumult of grief.

She would remain this way until her time would come to a close, and the tenuous power which brought her to this world was lost again. Lastly, he would watch her disappear into the dark, leaving him alone in the cold wet night.

As he stood with her now, he found it strange he should be relieved when she faded away. Each time the moment delayed longer an icy grip would seize him as he waited in horrified anticipation. He was afraid some grisly nightmare would play itself out before him. If her presence lasted too long, he might find himself watching her inevitable stumble and fall from the tower. And with every visit he steeled himself for the possibility he might be cursed to see his wife die in front of him, helpless to do anything but bear witness.

But the moment hadn't come. He began to hope his presence here was somehow holding back this inevitability. He knew this was likely not true. It was a silly hope. And while he was afraid to see this final moment, he had begun to realize he needed to see it. He could not bear the idea of her facing this a second time on her own. This was the true calling which brought him to this place each night. He must be there for her this time. He would not let her die alone, again.

His strength, so possessed of love and determination as it was, had nearly reached its limits. The illness was threatening to keep him from his unspoken promise. His heart would break if he had to abandon her out of weakness, betrayed by his own ailing and weakening form.

Then she turned to him. For the first time since she appeared last winter, she seemed to actually see him. He stepped away from her, nearly stumbling over the knee-high wall behind him. He steadied himself against the stone and gaped at her, wonder and fear swimming in his wide-eyed gaze. She had followed his movements, her eyes never leaving him.

Why now? For almost a year he had stood beside her, spoken to her, called out to her. Each night, without fail, he bore witness to the ongoing story unfolding in front of him while she played her part. Not one time had she acknowledged she was really there, that she was anything more than a reflection of something which had happened. Not once did she recognize him or show any sign she was aware of him at all. Until now.

Was it that night, the anniversary of her birth, which bestowed some additional power? Like the solstice before, which had broken the barriers so she might be visible to him, could there be a power on the day she was born into this world which finally broke the chains shackling her to the world beyond?

If this was true, did it mean she was not a prisoner to this nightly reenactment? Was she here because she chose to be? If so, then the obelisk was not her master, but simply the key to a power which allowed her to break through to the living world. She wasn't trapped here, reliving this horrible night, over and over again. She was coming here, to show him something.

"Was all of this for me?" His voice trembled as he spoke. There were so many thoughts shuffling chaotically through his mind, so many questions fighting for answers. The one thing he truly wanted to know was why. And then a thought came to him with such vivid clarity that he stood before her, his eyes looking deep into hers. She smiled gently as though she knew what he would ask next.

"Can you forgive me?"

No, this didn't feel right. He didn't feel like she was blaming him or condemning him for this failure. She didn't pass judgement on him; he was doing plenty of that already. And then it occurred to him it may be the guilt he had been carrying for her accident which was the reason for her appearances. He was dying, he knew that. Did she? Could it be she was here to relieve him of his burden of guilt?

It was the only truth he needed to know. He had cursed himself for decades for not being there when she wandered in her grief. It was his sad fate to exist in a world where she fell to her death while he had slept off his weariness in selfish laziness. This was the only question he had ever needed an answer for, but it was a question he was afraid to ask.

"Yes," was all she said. Somehow, he knew she was answering the unspoken question screaming in his mind. Then she turned back to the east. She stepped up onto the wall protecting them from the long drop. She tilted forward, looking downward into the sea crashing against the rocky shelf, reaching for her. She spread her arms wide as though to embrace the great empty chasm between herself and the jagged rocks which broke through the churning ocean below. Then she leaned out, accepting death as she disappeared into the fall.

It was the sudden realization this had always been the truth which filled the lightkeeper so thoroughly with anguish it burst from him in a heart-shattering cry. He reached out uselessly as she vanished, grasping only the night air. The undeniability of it was so clear to him. The lie he had been telling himself for so many years disintegrating in a single horrible moment.

He was suddenly liberated from years of guilt, only to have the vacancy filled with sour betrayal. Here he had witnessed her final moment, a reflection of time when she had given in to her grief. She had been taken by some madness, and she had abandoned him. In all those years since she threw herself from the tower, he had bestowed upon her memory a divine-like reverence. He had directed his devotion into the care given to this loveless, thoughtless, and cruel lighthouse. He made the tower his prison. This ugly and horrible thing was a monument to his guilt. His care for it had been the judgment by which he might atone for his failure.

He looked out at the obelisk, miles away above the sea. It was the uncaring architect of this hateful vision. If only it had left him to die with his guilt. Instead, it had taken what was likely the last days of his life and teased out this sad scene. While he was filled with a thunderstorm of emotions, the monolith simply stood floating above the water, a silent witness. And below the gleaming white tower was the ghastly reflection of the Finger of God, pointing back at him mockingly.

He turned from it, every muscle in his body tightening in furious rage. He saw the door for the hatch resting open on the stone floor and decided to leave this cursed tower forever. He took the stairs at a perilous speed, trying to escape as quickly as he could. He fled like a man possessed, running from the bitter truth, these new and horrifying revelations. He needed to be out of the lighthouse, away from this useless relic which had been a burden on his life for so long. He hated it. He cursed it. And he wanted to be free of it forever.

But he was old and sick, and the tower was dark and nearly lightless. He missed a step. Despite all the years traveling these stairs, knowing each brick, every crack in the mortar, every loose pebble and stone which was the skin and bones of this tower, he missed a step. His foot reached out and fell on open air. His body lurched forward. His arms windmilled in desperate and pointless panic. He slammed down on the stone with a fleshy smack and began to roll. He bounced down against the stone edges of the steps, the corners biting, cutting, and digging into his frail and sickly body. He couldn't cry out because each time he smashed into the next step the air was driven from him. His simply fell, again and again, until he was tossed onto the floor in a pathetic pile of battered bones and aching flesh.

He lay there, his body screaming in furious pain. The black fog of oblivion swam around him, closing in. He tried to crawl from it, heading to the next set of stairs which would bring him closer to his escape. He didn't want to die in this place. Not here, not in this tower.

But the fog had no care for his wants or needs. It gathered around him, growing cold and ever darker. It enveloped him, closing off the world, and pulling him into nothingness. His last conscious thought was a cold dark fear the lighthouse had done it. It had finally killed him.

Benjamin

On the morning of The Great Lamp Lighting, as the town had affectionately begun calling the impending farewell event for the lighthouse, Ben, and his wife Lilia, were hauling another load of donations to be added to the growing pile of fuel for the fire. They had proudly taken on the duties of administrating the town's newfound appreciation for the lighthouse. As they toddled down the main avenue with an overflowing handcart, they were greeted with warmth and excitement by the villagers rushing to finish any leftover business before the evening festivities. Some even followed with them, burdened by their own late additions for the fire. By the time they came to the final turn, they had adopted a group of about a dozen people heading toward the lighthouse.

The road came to a final turn and with a clumsy effort they began pushing the teetering cart up the last rise. Not far ahead the tower came into view, looming vacantly against a vibrant blue sky. A line of gulls sat noisily on the crown of gray stones calling out to each other. The growing mound was just barely visible above the top, beckoning the torch's flame.

In the shadow of the tower was a wide strip of flat and grassy shelf. It was close enough to get a good view of the event while being a respectful distance from the lightkeeper's hovel. On this soft field of green, a group of revelers were struggling to raise a series of brightly colored tents. They were losing a battle against the buffeting wind. They handled this with good spirits, laughing as a new gust came up and pulled the fabric away, dragging a pole or tie rope with it. A particularly nasty blast of wind took hold just as a large man was trying to secure one corner down to a stake in the ground. He was pulled backwards where he rolled awkwardly until his feet were kicking into the air. A small group of children laughed uproariously at this, while pointing and clapping. The large man seemed to give up, lying flat on his back, his belly bouncing up and down from his own laughter.

The day promised to be quite the unexpected holiday. A joyful feeling of celebration had spread contagiously through the village and nearby farms.

As the two pressed upwards with their ungainly burden their train of tagalongs broke off and headed for the area where the tents were failing to be raised. Loud and hearty greetings, a few cheers, and more laughter welcomed the newcomers. Many members of the crowd also called out and waved toward Ben and Lilia. Ben tried to wave back, nearly toppled the cart, and decided on a nod, large smile, and an abrupt "hello" instead. Lilia laughed at this and waved both her hands enthusiastically to make up for her husband's restricted reply.

It took some doing, but they were able to get the cart up the shell path, across the bridge, and up to the lighthouse door. The children watched with mischievous hopefulness, anticipating the soft path to be the couple's undoing. When the cart didn't topple the children cheered as a group, proudly applauding Ben's masterful handling of the precarious load. After he released the handles of the cart, he turned back to them, clasped his hands above his head and shook them in triumphant victory. The crowd of children cheered again, before finally returning to the ongoing comedy of the tent raising.

"Well, what do you think about that?" he asked Lilia. "I wasn't expecting all of this. It looks like they're setting up for a proper celebration."

She smiled back at him. "Well, people love the lighthouse."

"Of course they love it now," he said sardonically while looking back down the path. He turned back to her. "Do you think we're doing the right thing? I mean, retiring the lighthouse feels, I don't know, like we're giving up on her."

She wrapped her arms around him in a gentle embrace. The small swell of her belly pushed against him, reminding him of the life growing there, and his new responsibilities. "I think your uncle's right about this. The old tower doesn't really serve any purpose anymore. If the town really cares about it, they will find a way to take care of it on their own. You have your own family, and the mill, to think about now."

He sighed looking up at the tower, giving into the old logic once again. He rubbed her back as he returned the embrace. "You're right. You're both right. But if this old thing falls to ruin, I'm going to miss her."

"Me too," she agreed.

Reluctantly Ben released her and took the handles of the cart. Lilia, taking her cue, opened the door and held it for him. He negotiated the transition from the path to the stone floor of the lighthouse with surprising dexterity.

Nothing fell from the cart, and he slid the ungainly load straight through the door and into the inner chamber. Lilia arched her eyebrows with an exaggerated display of approval before closing the door.

It took a few moments for their eyes to adjust to the sudden gloom. This was routine and they both stood still until the room came into better focus. Ben headed for the staircase where they kept several wooden crates. These were used to transport the goods by hand up to the top of the tower. He handed one of the crates to Lilia and took another for himself before stopping abruptly. Something had caught his eye, something at the top of the stairs where they met the second floor. The color drained from his face, and the wooden crate fell from his suddenly numb hands. Lilia, turning at the sound of the wood crashing on the stone floor, called out to him.

"Ben, what's wrong?" she started to ask. He hardly heard her. He was flying up the stairs, taking the steps two at a time. She must have seen what he was heading for as she cried out, "Ben! Oh my..." her own crate crashed to the floor.

His uncle lay slumped against the wall at the top of the stairs, just passed the last step, almost hidden by shadow. A thin line of drying blood ran from under a clump of tangled hair, down his thin cheeks, and had fallen into a blooming stain across the front of his shirt. The old man was alive, but he either didn't hear his nephew calling out to him or couldn't respond. He was shivering, with his arms wrapped tightly around his chest for warmth. These arms, as well as his face, were covered in gray and purple bruises.

Ben knelt beside the old man and tried to rouse him. His uncle only muttered deliriously while trying to push away his nephew's probing hands. Then he erupted into a round of violent coughing. Ben could now see the black, tar-like, phlegm leaking from the corners of his mouth from other fits. After the outburst, the old man simply coiled back into his original position and resumed his mute shivering.

Lilia arrived, making the ascent more deliberately due to the child she carried inside her. "What happened?"

"It looks like he might have fallen down the steps. Maybe on the upper floors. I'm surprised he kept going afterwards and made it this far. Look at the cut on his head."

She looked it over carefully. The bleeding seemed to have stopped. "We need to get him into the house and clean this wound. He could do with some warming up too. You think he was here all night? It must have been freezing."

Ben lifted his uncle into his arms. The old man uttered only a small and whimpering sound. He tried to push his nephew away weakly, but Ben hardly noticed. He was surprised at how frail and light his uncle was now. He barely felt like he was holding a child. Ben could only wonder at how the old man had found the strength to climb the tower in the first place.

Carefully, they made their way down the stairs. Lilia took care of the door. Everything else, the cart and its collection of donations, were abandoned. They crossed the bridge and took the shell path to the hovel without being seen by the busy crowd setting up the celebration.

As they walked, Ben could hear a soft and weak muttering coming from his uncle. While he kept his eyes carefully glued to the path he was taking, he hazarded a momentary glance at the old man. The cold pallor of his uncle's face had softened a bit, seeming to have relaxed into a calm sleep. His eyes and cheeks were wet from fresh tears. What words the old man spoke were mumbled too quietly for Ben to understand. He had a feeling his uncle was talking to someone else, and Ben was quite certain he knew who the person might be.

Lilia went ahead to set the fireplace and got a kettle boiling. She had propped the rotting hovel door open for Ben, who only had to press his back against it slightly to make more room. He kicked away the prop holding the door, and it smacked itself closed behind him. The fire was just getting going, but it provided enough light to fill the room. Ben lay his uncle gently onto the bed and covered him with a torn blanket. He pulled the old man's battered chair next to the bed and sat down.

Lilia came over shortly, carrying a large bowl of clean water and some rags. She dipped one of the towels into the bowl and started to clean the old man's face.

"What happened?" she whispered to Ben.

"You don't have to whisper," he said. "I don't think we have to worry about waking him." She nodded but said nothing. After a moment Ben hazarded a guess. "It looks to me like he had taken a fall coming down the stairs last night."

"Why was he up in the tower at night?"

Ben wasn't sure how to answer. Old men had their secrets. Most were small little things, half forgotten. Some might even be unhealthy, or even dangerous. Ben's uncle always seemed like the kind of man to keep secrets. However, Ben couldn't think of anything the old man might hide which would be hurtful to himself, or anyone else. While he knew his uncle had been keeping something from him for quite a while now, he had chosen not to ask. He figured when it came down to it, his uncle would only give up the truth when he wanted to. Asking the old man wouldn't make a bit of difference.

He had, in fact, discovered the secret quite by accident.

Autumn – Part 2

Revelation

It was after one of his visits, a few weeks before, when Ben had stumbled onto a truth the lightkeeper was hiding from all of them. Ben had made several trips up the lighthouse to deposit the unwanted items they had sorted through in the storeroom. When he had returned to the hovel, he found his uncle had been dozing in his chair. Ben attempted to help him to his bed, but the old man woke up slightly, just enough to protest the intrusion.

"Unhand me, Benji. I can't go to bed now. She'll be here shortly, and I don't want to be sleeping." He was clearly still partly asleep, but there was a gentle earnestness in his voice. Ben abandoned the effort and looked around for something to cover the old man. He could, at least, keep the old man from catching a chill.

"Who's coming, uncle?" he asked absently while covering the old man with the blanket from the bed.

"Your aunt. She comes at night, in the dark." He had seemed to fall back into a dreamlike state. His eyes were closed, and his head hung limply against his chest. His voice had a distant, almost drunklike quality to it.

"Oh, and what happens when she comes?" Ben asked. He liked hearing about his aunt, even if it were only a dream.

"She sings. And we walk to the tower. We'll stand and look at the sea."

"And then what happens?"

"She leaves."

"Where does she go?"

"Away," it came as a sad whisper. Ben decided against pressing further.

It was getting very late. Ben didn't want to leave his uncle here like this, lying slumped in a chair with only a blanket over him. He wondered if he should stay with him. The old man didn't look comfortable. But he had gotten so little sleep lately, Ben was reluctant to disturb what rest he was getting now. He could get a small fire going to help warm the place, and if his uncle slumped out of the chair, he'd be there to help him out. But he had no way of getting word to Lilia, who might worry when her husband had not returned by morning.

He decided he should wake his uncle. It was possible to wake him just enough to climb into the bed, where he might just fall right back to sleep. Ben stepped next to him, put a hand behind his shoulder, and lightly pressed him forward while calling to him in a soft voice. The old man woke up gently, blinking away the sleep and looking around with a touch of embarrassment on his face.

"Oh, I must have dozed off. What's the hour, Benji?"

"Late, I think. I hated to wake you, Uncle. But you didn't look very comfortable sleeping in that old chair." The old man stood up, stretched, and stifled a deep yawn.

"Nonsense." He looked out the window, seemed to find what he was looking for, and then he turned back to his nephew. "So, I guess you'll be on your way then?"

"Well, I was hoping, since it's so late, I might just stay here. I could sleep on the chair. If it's alright with you of course."

The lightkeeper looked back toward the window. He looked unsure, almost nervous. "No, no. You should be getting back. That wife of yours will be worried enough as it is." He headed to the door and opened it. Ben was surprised his uncle was rushing him out so abruptly. Perhaps the old man was still caught in his own dream, expecting a visit from his late wife. It seemed absurd, but the illness was getting worse. Could it be affecting his mind now?

"Uncle, I think I should…" The look on his uncle's face stopped him cold. There was the determination in his eyes Ben had seen numerous times before. He had ignored this same look on his uncle's face before and found himself on the wrong side of the old man's surprisingly fierce anger. Understanding the futility of continuing to argue, he changed course. "Alright, alright. If you say so. I'll be back in a few days to take some more of the storeroom items to the top."

"Yes, yes. I'll see you in a few days," the old man said. By now, he was all but pushing Ben through the door. Ben had barely crossed the threshold when the door slammed closed, and he heard the latch clasp on the other side. For a moment Ben hesitated. He almost rapped on the door, but he took a breath and thought better of it.

He started the lonely march home in the dark. The moon was bright and nearly full, and the cloudless sky was filled with brilliant starlight. Under the dim glow of the night sky, he had very little trouble making his way through the quiet and empty village. As he walked his mind kept returning to his uncle, and the unsettling hesitation he felt at the door began to grow, pulling against him like a leash.

He had made it almost halfway when the nagging thoughts haunting him won out. He stopped in the middle of the street, staring down at his feet for several moments, wondering what was upsetting him so fiercely about the last exchange with the old man. Finally, he gave in to his troubled feelings, turned, and headed back to the lighthouse.

Several times on his way back he nearly turned around again. He wasn't quite sure what he would do when he got back to the hovel. He couldn't even explain the deepening concern which was growing inside him. There was just a need to return, a tightening of a leash which was pulling him with an ever-growing determination. His uncle's words kept echoing over and over in his mind, "We'll stand and look at the sea."

He had made the last turn and was coming up the rise. The lighthouse looked like nothing more than a black absence of starlight. The moon was behind it, causing a great darkness to cast over the path and the house. It was because of this long shadow he did not see his uncle. But he did hear the old man's footsteps crunching loudly on the shell path as they were heading away from the hovel toward the lighthouse.

Ben stepped onto the grass, hoping to conceal the sounds of his own footsteps. He continued up, following the path, until he was finally able to see his uncle. The old man walked in silence, yet he kept turning to his left, and when he did, he would slow down as if looking or listening for something. Ben froze when he did this, but it took only a few seconds before his uncle would resume his normal pace.

When the old man arrived at the lighthouse, he opened the door and entered the dark lower chamber. Ben followed quietly. The door to the lighthouse had not been closed completely, so he was able to push it open softly and without much noticeable noise. Inside, he saw nothing. Only thin streams of light pierced through the darkness, stabbing through the empty room. Remembering his uncle's sleepy words, Ben started up the stairs.

He walked slowly, trying not to make a sound. He could hear the slow shuffle of the old man's footsteps climbing up the stairs. Then he heard his uncle say something. He couldn't make it out, but he was clearly speaking to someone. Ben heard the trap door, which led to the crown of the tower, squeal open on its old and rusted hinges. It slammed against something with a loud and heavy thud, followed by the howling wind blowing across the tower's parapet. Ben continued his climb to the top, more quickly now that he was confident the wind would conceal his footsteps. He found the hatch left open and peered out into the night air.

The pile of treasures was still small. The town had only begun to spread the rumor of the lighthouse's last lighting, and there were only the few unkept items from the storeroom which had been piled on the crown. Ben could see clearly around the shallow mound while standing at the opening at the top of the stairs. His uncle was alone on the eastern side of the crown, facing the sea.

"We'll stand and look at the sea," echoed in Ben's mind.

Then the old man turned to his left, looking south, but not toward the obelisk. The obelisk was much further out across the water in the east. It would be only a few more months before it would finally vanish across the horizon. No, he was looking at something he saw right in front of him, something he was speaking to.

Ben sighed. So, this was why the old man slept in so late each morning. He had been keeping himself awake so he could imagine walking with his wife to the top of the tower.

Ben wondered if this had been a common thing for them. Would they often come out here at night together, to gaze at the stars or stare out at the sea? Was the old man remembering these times, or reliving them in a strange and mad illusion? He suddenly wanted to put a stop to this. He wanted to confront the old man and show him he was imagining things.

But was he? Within the mind of his uncle, this might be real. It was clear enough to him, based on what had happened in the hovel earlier, his uncle seemed to believe his wife was coming to him in the night. Even while awake the old man was pushing Ben away lest he be there when the hallucination began. If he challenged the old man about this, would he be exposing some sad delusion, or destroying a dying man's last fantasy?

Ben was a caring man, who believed keeping his uncle happy was more important than exposing some truth. In the end, he should at least make a decision with some thought behind it, rather than bursting in and interrupting the old man in some rash display of unwanted reason. Resolving to have a good and long think over the matter, Ben grudgingly descended the stairs and headed for home, leaving his uncle to his imaginary visit. This time he made it home, where his wife was indeed quite worried about him.

Understanding

"**Y**ou never told me about this," Lilia said. She turned away from him, putting her attention back to caring for the old man. Her face had darkened somewhat, and her eyes narrowed in troubled thought. Ben could see having kept this from her had hurt her.

"It wasn't my secret, Lilia," he tried to explain. It felt like a flimsy excuse, but it was the honest truth. "I wasn't meant to see him like that. I felt like I might be betraying him if I said anything. Besides, I never thought it would come to any harm. I surely never expected this."

Lilia seemed to understand, at least a little. She would have to. If Ben had said anything about this, she may have insisted they do something about the nightly walks. On the other hand, she may have had some advice or insight he could have used. His uncle always said she was clever, and Ben had been a fool to disregard this truth.

Ultimately, Ben chose to struggle with this privately. He decided to take his chances on saying and doing nothing, hoping his uncle would have given up the night walks after he had gotten too weak. Clearly, Ben had been mistaken.

Then Lilia did something Ben had not expected. She started singing quietly, almost to herself. It was a lullaby, something he hadn't heard since he was a child. It was a soft and soothing song, often sung to children to comfort and calm them when they were unwell or afraid.

As she sang, she continued to wipe the blood, dirt, and filth from the old man's face. Slowly the color came back to his cheeks, and he appeared to be coming back to life as the ugliness was literally being washed away. A strange sort of calm fell over him. His mouth softened into a light and sleepy smile. The great and bushy brows, which had been smashed together in a tight and painful looking furrow, relaxed into soft arches which pulled the cracks and wrinkles away from his forehead and the corners of his eyes. Years of sorrow and pain seemed to fall away from the old man's face.

The song faded into its last notes. One of the old man's hands reached up. Lilia took it with both of hers and kissed the knuckles softly. His uncle took a deep and cleansing breath. His eyes half opened, and he seemed to be looking at Lilia.

"I'm sorry. I'm so sorry," he whispered. "I didn't know. If I only knew, could I have done something? What could I have done to keep you from leaving me? What could I have done to stop you from jumping?" His face was pleading. Tears filled his eyes and fell silently to the pillow. He closed his eyes, but the tears kept falling.

Lilia looked to her husband, surprise and confusion screaming from her silent expression. She was pleading to him with those eyes, looking for understanding. Ben leaned in close, his voice dropping to a low whisper.

"He's talking to my aunt. Their child was born lifeless. Not long after, she jumped from the top of the lighthouse. I didn't think he believed it, but I guess he's finally accepted she killed herself."

"What do you mean? How do you know she killed herself?" she whispered. She still hadn't looked back at the old man. Her eyes were fixed on Ben.

"My mother talked about it. After my aunt lost the baby, she had gotten sick. She wouldn't eat or drink for days. They had to force drink and food when they could, broth and soup mostly. And sometimes, she would just get up and leave. My mother would find her walking to the lighthouse, or even climbing the stairs. The only times she ever spoke was when my mother caught her doing this. She dragged my aunt back to the bed. She would resist, pulling away from my mother. And sometimes she would cry out 'Let me go,' or 'I need to be with my baby.'" Ben looked mournfully at his uncle.

"Why didn't anyone tell him?" Lilia asked.

"I'm sure they tried. But I don't think he wanted to know. He always avoided it. We never really talked about it as I got older. But when we did, he always called it 'her accident.'"

"It sounds to me like he blames himself."

Ben didn't know what to say to that. He had only been a child at the time. Now, with fatherhood arriving soon for him, imagining the loss of his own child was too horrifying. What could he do to help Lilia if the same thing were to happen? What would she do? He shut out the thoughts quickly.

Lilia

ilia couldn't have known, but her own mind was traveling along the same pathways as Ben's. Unlike her husband, she didn't shut the thoughts away. She opened herself to them, following their tangent paths to all the devastating horrors they led to.

Lilia accepted she could not relate fully to Ben's aunt. The pain was uniquely hers. Even a mother could only imagine such tragedy. Lilia also knew every mother would bear such loss in their own private way. Heaven forbid Lilia should ever know such pain. But even if she did, it would not be the same pain Ben's aunt had suffered. It would be solely Lilia's personal heartbreak. Its wound would be unique to her, and what it might do to her own mind may be greater, or lesser. How it healed, or if it ever could, would be entirely up to Lilia. Ben would be no more than a silent witness to her suffering.

And with that tentative brush against the pain of their tragedy, Lilia believed she had found some truth, and a bitter understanding.

She turned to the lightkeeper. One of her hands released the old man's and she brushed back the hair which had matted against his face. What she did next caused Ben to abandon the chair he was sitting in as he sank to his knees beside her. Lilia spoke softly and deliberately. Her voice taking a tone she did not recognize.

"It was never your fault. There was nothing you could do. She loved you more than anything, and she would never have left you. She was lost, so very lost, and she couldn't find her way home. The darkness surrounding her had hidden you from her. She wandered in the darkness looking for a light, looking for a way back to you, and she fell. She fell trying to find her way back to you."

Fall

The Lighthouse

The afternoon was settling into evening and there had been no sign of the lightkeeper, his nephew, or the nephew's wife. This hadn't discouraged the villagers' merry making. At best, their absence elicited some idle questions which were little more than conversation starters.

"Have you seen the keeper?"

"No, I haven't. I'm looking forward to the lighting though."

"Me too. What a wonderful idea to celebrate this..." and on it would go.

The celebration had evolved into a proper fair day event. Several tents had been raised. There were some stories and a bit of laughter as the revelers recounted their battle against the seaside wind which had provided quite the challenge in assembling the tents. Now that they were safely erected, they provided quite the selection of festive fun. There were tables laden with food of all sorts, including sweets, cakes, ham, fish and other cooked meats, fruits, and a spread of fresh vegetables. The children ignored the latter part and, to the chagrin of their parents, absolutely devoured the cakes and sweets almost as fast as they could be displayed.

One tent had become the unofficial tavern, as it stored the various kegs of ale, mead, and crates filled with bottles of wine. The innkeepers had provided the libations from their own storerooms. As such, they felt personally responsible for maintaining the flow of drink in a fashion best regulated through their management. Never missing an opportunity to turn a coin, the innkeepers were the only ones to charge for their goods during the event. No one seemed to grumble about this, and the innkeepers' purses grew fat and heavy throughout the celebration. Many of the more practical wives were quite happy to take advantage of the rigid dedication to commerce. It gave them ample opportunity to temper their husband's enthusiasm for drink by holding on to the family purse with almost miserly restraint. There was some grumbling, but also fewer drunken fist fights as a result.

Another tent provided space for games and dancing. Cheerful music drifted out from the colorful canopy and filled the yard outside with its quick rhythm and melodic notes. The sharp steps and stomps of dancing feet on makeshift wooden floors were keeping respectable time with the songs being played. Dancing wasn't reserved for the tents, and more than a few lucky (or unlucky depending on the case) girls were scooped up into a whirlwind of fast feet and flowing skirts.

As the afternoon faded, and evening claimed a darkening sky, torches and small fires were lit to provide some light for the party. People began to talk more earnestly about the missing lightkeeper. One of the bakers, the father-in-law to the lightkeeper's nephew, was elected to check the keeper's hovel and find out what they had in mind for the coming lighting.

In truth, the baker had been quite concerned his daughter and her husband had been absent from the entire celebration. He could expect their tardiness due to some last-minute preparations. But their absence had gone on far longer than was appropriate. Any conversation he had with Lilia over the past few days led him to believe the lighting ceremony should have already gotten under way. Therefore, he gladly accepted the responsibility for no other reason than to alleviate his concerns for his daughter. And so, without further encouragement, he headed to the hovel.

As he drew closer to the small house, he could see the windows had been shuttered closed. However, thin lines of orange light peaked through the edges and between the cracks of the wood shutters. He heard no sounds from the house, but he continued without much concern. When he arrived at the door, he knocked lightly against the decrepit rotten wood.

Ben answered the door. His face was drawn and haggard and he looked exhausted. A moment of confusion washed from his eyes when he recognized Lilia's father. Ben opened the door without a word. Lilia was sitting in a chair next to a bed. The lightkeeper was lying in it, seemingly asleep. Lilia looked up, saw her father, and rose immediately to greet him. The baker could clearly see what was happening and raised a hand to quiet her before she would try to explain. Instead, he looked to Ben, his eyes filled with genuine concern.

"I'm sorry, lad. Is he...did he?" he stammered. No one ever accused the baker of being a wise man, but at this particular moment he felt like an absolute fool. Everyone knew the old lightkeeper was very ill, and he had been wasting away for some time. No small amount of idle talk was spent wondering how much longer till the old man finally shoved off and cast away from this mortal coil. And yet, he couldn't find a simple or tactful way of finishing his sentence. Few people were comfortable talking about death as it was. Speaking the word to the old man's single remaining family member had baffled the old baker's conversation skills. Luckily, Ben was cleverer than he looked.

"No, no. He's just asleep. He took quite a fall last night. We found him this morning and have been caring for him today."

"I see. Well, I guess that puts an end to things for tonight then." He looked with pity at the old man in the bed but did not attempt to intrude or enter the house. "I'll leave you to care for him. I'll be back to see if there's anything I can do to help. In the meantime, I'll tell everyone the lighting has been put off for now."

"The lighting." Ben said. His voice was filled with the kind of reluctant acceptance one might have for a chore they would prefer to put off.

"It's a shame he didn't get to see how folks made a fuss over the old thing. Might have done him some good, I think. Warm his heart I'd bet. Shame this is."

Lilia looked at Ben with an expression of sympathy. Ben responded with only stoic silence.

"Hold on a moment, Da'," Lilia said. Her father had just turned to leave but stopped and looked at her expectantly. She had turned her attention to Ben. "You don't really have to, you know that."

"No, I really do." He responded defeatedly. "I'll grab my jacket and a lantern." He turned to gather his things before Lilia could protest.

"What? Don't be silly. Your uncle needs you now, Ben. These folk will understand."

"It's not that, Da'. It's her birthday today." The confused look on her father's face took her back for a second. Then she explained. "The lighthouse belonged to Ben's aunt." She gestured to the lighthouse keeper asleep in the bed. "His late wife. They had chosen her birthday to be the day of the last lighting. It's important to them it be done today."

"Ah, I see." It seemed to him like a touching gesture. It was sad the old man would sleep through it. But then a new thought occurred to him. "What about the lightkeeper? If he wakes up, he'll not see it."

Lilia seemed to be the only one to hear him. She looked around the room, picked one of the windows, and cast open its shutters. There, silhouetted against the growing night, was the tower. She looked back at the old man in the bed and frowned. Her father understood and saw the solution.

Ben was starting to leave. He was wearing his jacket, and he carried an old and battered lantern in one hand. The baker grabbed his arm as he made his escape out the door. "Hold a minute, lad. I'll need your help with the bed," he said while pulling Ben back inside. For a moment, Ben only looked at the baker with a confused expression. Then he saw his wife by the open window, the only open window, which faced the lighthouse. The baker was now at the foot of the old man's bed and Ben suddenly understood what was needed.

Ben handed the lantern to Lilia and grabbed the head of the bed. The baker nodded from his end and grabbed the bed posts. They counted off, and gently lifted the bed, with the keeper still laying on it, wrapped in the ragged blankets. With Lilia guiding them, they set it back down in the middle of the room where the old man's face could look right through the window and onto the crown of the lighthouse if he should wake.

Ben smiled up at the baker. "Thank you for this."

The baker smiled and stood next to his daughter. "'Twas nothing, lad. Now, get on and set a fire up there. Folks is waiting."

Indeed, they were. When the young man left the house carrying the light a great cheer could be heard from the celebration below. Lilia and her father, followed Ben outside. He was holding the lantern up and waving to the crowd. Then he turned back to his wife, flashed an awkward smile, kissed her cheek, and turned back to the lighthouse.

They watched Ben from just outside the front door of the hovel as he crossed the bridge and entered the tower. The soft glow of the lantern flickered fleetingly through the windows as he climbed his way to the top. There was nothing but restrained silence from the festive crowd, and all was quiet. Only the gentle hum of the sea wind and the flapping of the tent cloth could be heard. Lilia followed the glow of the lamp as Ben ascended the final floor and onto the top of the crown.

Several minutes of silence accompanied the wavering glow of the lamp as the onlookers waited. Nothing seemed to happen. A murmur started to whisper through the confused crowd as they stared up into the black shadow of the tower. Then there was a soft bloom of orange light. It shuddered and danced for a few seconds before a bright lick of yellow flame shot out of the top of the tower. It looked in that moment like a great stone candle. The pile caught then, and more flames joined the first. Soon a great conflagration blossomed and filled the crown. The fire was great, its light full and vibrant. Suddenly, the torches and little fires set earlier to light the festivities below were made useless as the glow from the tower became nearly as bright as day.

Applause leapt from the crowd. Cheers and shouts followed. The musicians struck up another lively tune and the children started to run in circles and dance. Toasts were made and heavy tankards of drink were drained in huge gulps. Then the voices of the crowd joined in a song which filled Lilia's heart. She hugged her father tightly and watched the light of Ben's lantern descend the lighthouse for the last time.

Benjamin

That night Ben was enjoying his second cup of coffee in his uncle's worn and battered chair when the old man finally woke up. The room was bright, filled with the glow coming from the lighthouse. His uncle got up, slowly sliding his legs around to the side of the bed and stared at the open window facing the tower for several minutes. He suddenly seemed aware his bed had been moved and looked around the room curiously. Ben waited for the old man to finish his scan of the hovel without a word. When his gaze fell on his nephew, he smiled weakly and then turned back to the window.

"I see you lit the old girl." The statement was dry and matter of fact. Ben wasn't entirely sure if there was an accusation, or some other emotion simmering under those words. His empty tone still seemed to want a reply, or an explanation.

"I didn't want to miss her birthday," he uttered apologetically. It was all he could think to say.

"You did the right thing, Benji. It warms my heart to see the fire up there. Thank you," his uncle said. His voice was still dry, and weak. Ben understood now the tonelessness was simply because it was difficult for the old man to talk. Despite the dryness, there was a warmth, hidden inside the low voice. It was a relief to hear the old man agreed with his actions. A small part of him had been afraid his uncle would be upset the lighthouse ceremony continued without him.

The old man coughed. It was weak, wet, and choked. He grabbed a rag from the bowl left by his bed, wiped his face with it. He started to get up. Ben leaned out to stop him, but the old man looked at him sharply, silently telling him not to interfere. Ben sat back down, watching the old man carefully, ready to spring into action if he should stumble, or worse.

His concern was unwarranted. The old man got up slowly, testing his own strength and winced at the pain. Once he was standing, he took a few deep breaths, his eyes pressed closed. After a few seconds, his eyes opened, and he walked to the open window. Standing there, with the glow of the lighthouse's fire shining down on him, he looked down at his stained shirt, examined the bruises on his arms, and gingerly touched the cut on his head. Then he looked at his nephew, his face filled with a hundred questions.

"Lilia and I found you in the lighthouse this morning. It looks like you had an accident." He didn't want to suggest anything more than that. He didn't need to. His uncle simply nodded in understanding.

"I'm sorry to have caused so much trouble. I hope I wasn't too much of a bother."

"No, Uncle. You don't have to worry about it. I'm just glad we found you." His uncle looked at him long and hard. Finally, he seemed to accept this and didn't press on.

Then his face tightened and paled with sudden panic. "What time is it?" he snapped sharply.

"It's just after midnight. You can relax a moment. There's still plenty of time." Ben hoped his tone was soothing. It seemed to do the trick. The old man sat down on the bed again and looked back at his nephew.

"I see," he said softly.

"Do you need help with the stairs?"

The old man seemed to think about it for a moment. Then he shook his head. "I have to go alone."

"I thought you might say that." Ben got up and poured a cup of coffee for his uncle and handed it to him. He took a seat next to the old man. They drank their cups in silence, looking out of the window, watching the lighthouse burn. Ben accepted the quiet. Part of him understood there wouldn't be many good or quiet times for the two of them together. The illness had all but taken his uncle, and as it continued things would become more difficult. If so, Ben could think of no better memory than sitting in the hovel with him, drinking coffee, and watching the lighthouse fire burn full and bright.

The Keeper

His body was a symphony of sore muscles, painful bruises, and aching joints. His head was filled with tiny hammers, pounding away at his temple, trying to blast the front of his skull into a thousand pieces. The cut on the side of his head burned acidly. The pain seemed miles away.

He sipped at his coffee absently, watching the fire burn high upon the stone crown of the lighthouse. He really didn't care that he missed the ceremony. That had been for Benji's benefit. But watching it now, to see the light once again, should have brought home some kind of emotion. He felt only emptiness. All he could think of was the wooden toy soldier, scarred, chipped, and chewed. He imagined it being consumed in the fire.

Time slipped by while he sat lost in the light. Then Benji stood up, breaking the spell. The lightkeeper was grateful for the interruption to his thoughts.

"Well, Uncle. I think it's time I get on home." The old man got up. Ben took the cup from the old man and handed him his walking stick and the key to the tower. Nothing was said. There was no explanation. He wasn't sure what the boy knew, or how he knew it. He was simply glad there was an understanding. He embraced the boy, who returned the hug silently.

They left the hovel together. Outside they bid each other their normal farewells. Nothing else needed to be said. The old man watched as Benji started down the path which led him to the main road. When the boy got to the end of the intersection, he turned, waved back at the old man, and then headed toward home.

The lightkeeper turned to face the tower, the normally gray stone now reflecting a golden light from the flame above. All the hurts were much more present now. But even the crushing physical pain seemed slight compared to what had really hurt him last night. Watching his wife's suicide, coming to terms with the realization she had abandoned him, and learning he had spent his life in service to a false memory was devastating. The rage and pain had seemed to exist outside of him. The monstrous storm of emotion had nearly consumed him. It had nearly killed him.

It seemed sleep had sobered him. The delusionary phantoms which assaulted him last night had been exorcised. He saw the lighthouse for what it was now, a heaping collection of stone and nostalgia. It had no power, or malice. It was not the architect of his endless labor. Nor was it his wife's executioner. It was simply a sad and useless pile of stone, fittingly being retired to the ravages of an unknown future. A future he knew lay far beyond his own.

He wondered if he could make the climb again. He didn't think she would return tonight. The revelation seemed to be the point of her visits, and the secret was now unlocked. His eyes started to burn at the corners as tears threatened to fall. He was surprised by this sadness. He wanted to be angry with her. He wanted to be free from her.

She was lost, so very lost, and she couldn't find her way home.

It seemed like a random and foreign thought, not his own, but an idle thing passing across a swirl of confused emotions. It pierced through the fog with such vivid confidence he knew it must be true. It was like a new awakening. Memories came back to him bringing new illumination. He stared at the tower with vacant, empty eyes. The blazing fire at the crown drew him deep into the past, burning away the fog of time with sad lucidity.

It came to him like a waking dream. The pain of their child, born silent, lifeless, and unbreathing. He grieved for their loss while fighting futilely to save his wife as she wasted away in grief. The world kept turning, oblivious to her suffering as she withered away, growing frail and thin. Soon, the only difference between his wife and their lost child, was her weakening breath.

The darkness which surrounded her had hidden you from her.

He had managed to feed her broth and water. It seemed to help. The thin food began to nourish her. She would sit up at times, awake, but still dreaming. She was an empty participant in her recovery. She would sit limply and lethargically, responding to her husband as he nursed her back to health with a wordless imitation of life.

Then, one morning, he woke to find her bed empty. He searched for her until discovering her broken body on the rocks below the lighthouse. She was just below their spot, the spot where they would stand together before an endless sea and an infinite sky. He wanted to think she had wandered there in her delirium and fell. He wanted to believe this was an accident.

She wandered in the darkness looking for a light, looking for a way back to you, and she fell.

This was the truth. He didn't even care if it was real. It was a truth he wanted, he needed to accept. She had betrayed him no more than he had failed her. For the first time since he had found her body, he was glad he had spent all those many years keeping the lighthouse. For if it had fallen into ruin, he would never have known the truth.

He traveled the path of crushed shells slowly. He savored each step. Even the pain in his bruised legs could not spoil the growing sense of completeness filling him with each footfall. He opened the door to the tower, entered the dark chamber, closed, and locked the door behind him. He turned and stood before the stairs. The stone stairs would not challenge him. He held no fear of them. He placed the key in his pocket, took a deep breath, and stepped forward. He took each step with a slow and cautious pace. He would not fall. No corner would turn a mislaid foot. The strain was immense. His weakening legs struggled with the effort as he climbed. But he refused to waver, and through iron determination he ascended the tower, his eyes fixed ever upward, looking for the soft glow of the firelight.

The warmth of the crown came to him first. He closed his eyes and stretched his old and weathered face toward it, letting it pull him forward. He came to the trap door and pushed. It was heavier than he remembered. His broken and diseased body, a vessel barely fit to hold onto life, the dying husk he had become no longer had the strength to raise the hatch.

He refused to allow his weakness to stop him. Death would come, this was certain. It was reaching out for him, and he had known it for days. But he would meet death on his terms, his way, with her standing beside him. He prayed to the unseen power of the obelisk to allow it, to give him this one concession. Grant him this simple dying wish.

He pushed again. He put everything he had left into it. The old muscles, bruised, aching, and nearly used up, screamed angrily. He refused their cries. He pressed upward, stepping forward as he pressed against the hatch. The slab of wood planks bound together with pitted iron braces began to give way. The rusted hinges shrieked, joining the chorus of his raging sinews. He cried out against the pain, but he pushed. A gap opened and grew wider. Warmth, light, and salty sea air mixed with the stench of burning wood. Slowly, the door reached the apex of its arch and fell away from him, crashing against the stone floor.

The massive heat of the bonfire slammed into him as he staggered out of the hole onto the stone floor of the crown. He crawled to the parapet and pulled himself up onto the edge. He sat for a moment, the great heat of the inferno pressing against him like a living thing. After the throbbing of his aching legs calmed themselves enough for him to continue, he stood up and began to walk along the edge of the crown, keeping his hand lightly resting on the crenelated wall in case his legs should betray him.

They did not. He made it to the eastern side, where he saw her, waiting for him.

She watched him approach with sad and sympathetic eyes. He took his place beside her, barely standing, gasping for breath. The smoke had filled the air and his damaged lungs didn't have the strength to power a single word. He wanted to say he forgave her. He wanted her to forgive him. More than anything, he just wanted to tell her he loved her. She smiled at him, as though he had managed to say the words, and she had heard him.

He knew what must come next. The tower, and its stairs, had become an impassible barrier. His body would not survive the descent. And what if he could make the climb? Would he then spend his last moments, or days, watching what was left of his wretched carcass waste away as his disease consumed him? Would his nephew watch him die in a sickbed filled with the putrid stench of his decay? He saw no path down those stairs which allowed him any dignity in death. There was nothing down there but pain and suffering.

Before him, stood an apparition of his love, his wife. She was no less real to him at that moment than she was all those years ago, when they stood here while she still lived. But he was afraid. The unknowable fate before him, when death would finally claim its prize, brought to him the same cold terror which filled all men who face the end of their mortality. Her presence offered some hope, though slim it may be, for there was still some lingering doubt this was a fiction created by the power of the obelisk.

He was a man who knew no god, but he still wanted to believe there was a place for them beyond this world. A place where they could still be together. It need not be a paradise, or heaven. But could it just exist? Could there be one single blessing for him? He had to hope. He was all but dead now, a broken shell, barely able to stand, rotting from the inside. Only time and fear were holding him here.

She took his hand, and he felt it. He never wanted to be denied her touch. And then it occurred to him it didn't matter what lay beyond. It didn't matter if this was the obelisk's illusion. If he were to die, he would choose now, next to her, with her. And whatever would come, if even nothing at all would follow, it would be enough.

He stepped onto the wall, and she stepped up beside him.

Together, they opened their arms to embrace the night.

He leaned his head back, lifting his face to the star-filled sky. The heat from the fire pressed against his back. All the pain was gone. He breathed in the cold, clean, night air.

He leaned forward.

And together they fell.

A Word from the Author

And so, dear reader, we conclude the first of many stories concerning the fate of the people caught in the strange and mysterious aura of The Monolith. Although you may feel that this story ended sadly, I hope that you will still find that there was some joy, and love, hidden within this final trial of the lighthouse keeper.

As with many of my stories, this one was brought to life while sitting with my children, telling stories over coffee. Grace seemed particularly taken with this sad story. It was due to her enthusiasm that this became the first of The Monolith Series stories, though I had intended it to be the last.

There are many other stories to tell. I can't promise to be any more illuminating on the subject of the obelisk's nature, purpose, or origin. I'm afraid what is happening to the people in its wake are far more interesting to me. I hope that this will not disappoint you too much.

As I continue to chronicle these strange tales, please take a moment to rate and review this story on whatever platform you acquired it on. Independent authors, such as me, depend on these reviews to help other readers find our stories. Please share this story with friends or family you think may also find this entertaining.

Finally, to track my progress, or yell or scream at me for whatever reason, please follow me on various social media platforms. You can find links to these on my website at www.ruelknudson.com. I am doing much better at being engaged with the socials and you are likely to find I am quite interactive. You can also join my mailing list where you will find opportunities to get advanced digital copies of my stories ahead of release.

I continue to hope that we will meet again, at the end of yet another story.